A Gypsy's Book of Revelation

A Gypsy's Book

of

REVELATION

stories

Cécile Barlier

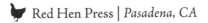 Red Hen Press | *Pasadena, CA*

This book is the Winner of the 2019 Grace Paley Prize in Short Fiction. AWP is a national nonprofit organization dedicated to serving American letters, writers, and programs of writing. AWP's headquarters are at Riverdale Park, Maryland.

Book Design by Mark E. Cull

Library of Congress Cataloging-in-Publication Data

Names: Barlier, Cécile, 1971– author.
Title: A gypsy's book of revelation : stories / Cécile Barlier.
Description: Pasadena, CA : Red Hen Press, [2021]
Identifiers: LCCN 2020049840 | ISBN 9781888996876 (trade paperback) | ISBN 9781888996920 (epub)
Subjects: LCGFT: Short stories.
Classification: LCC PS3602.A77558 G97 2021 | DDC 813/.6—dc23
LC record available at https://lccn.loc.gov/2020049840

The National Endowment for the Arts, the Los Angeles County Arts Commission, the Ahmanson Foundation, the Dwight Stuart Youth Fund, the Max Factor Family Foundation, the Pasadena Tournament of Roses Foundation, the Pasadena Arts & Culture Commission and the City of Pasadena Cultural Affairs Division, the City of Los Angeles Department of Cultural Affairs, the Audrey & Sydney Irmas Charitable Foundation, the Meta & George Rosenberg Foundation, the Albert and Elaine Borchard Foundation, the Adams Family Foundation, Amazon Literary Partnership, the Sam Francis Foundation, and the Mara W. Breech Foundation partially support Red Hen Press.

First Edition
Red Hen Press
www.redhen.org

Acknowledgments

Thank you to the editors of the following publications in which these stories first appeared.

Amarillo Bay, (May 2013): "The Door Test"; *The Delmarva Review* 9, (2016): "Immersion"; *The Emerson Review* 45, (Spring 2016): "Pisces"; *Gone Lawn,* no. 33 (Summer 2019): "Home"; *The Meadow,* (Summer 2018): "Rêve"; *New Delta Review,* (November 2012): "Swallowing Carolyn"; *Red Savina Review* 6, no. 1 (Spring 2018): "MRI"; *Saint Anne Review,* (Winter 2015): "Polish Dusk"; *Serving House Journal,* no. 9 (Spring 2014): "Wednesdays of the Japanese Wave"; *Sou'wester,* (Fall 2015): "Immersion"; *The Summerset Review,* (Fall 2017): "The Point of No Return"; *The Tower Journal,* (Spring 2013): "Full of Grace"; and *Valparaiso Fiction Review* 5, no. 1 (Winter 2015): "The Bond."

"Forgetting" was featured in *The Lindenwood Review,* no. 4 (2014), in *The Writers Studio at 30* (Epiphany Editions, 2017), and was nominated for the Pushcart Prize.

"A Gypsy's Book of Revelation" was featured in *Cerise Press* 5, no. 13 (Summer 2013) and was nominated for the Pushcart Prize.

"Legionnaire" was featured in *Bacopa* (2012) and won first place for fiction.

Contents

A Gypsy's Book of Revelation

A Gypsy's Book of Revelation

Picture number one: I lay in a box and rest. Forever. I thought Western science would find some clever way to dispose of my body. It turns out Western science doesn't attend to the dead, and so I end up impaled on the horns of a dilemma like Manolete on the horns of a bull: I rot or I get burned; either way I end up in a container. Whether this or the other has been the subject of many late-night talks with my daughter Yelena: *Well, Mamita, you can't have it both ways.* "Why not?" I say, because "Why not?" is in my blood—or was. In the end I choose fire because I can be burnt in their midst, and rotting is a lonely enterprise.

Picture number two: the crematorium is a plain building painted in white. The whiteness of it makes my children squint their eyes under the noon sun. I am not driven in a hearse; I am walked there; my box held high on their shoulders. It hits me that dead bodies are walked just like dogs are walked, depending on our beloved for just a sniff of air. Luckily, it wouldn't occur to my children to drive me through the crematorium any more than through a coffee shop or a pharmacy. We're not a drive-through people and we're late.

We squish together through the bare wooden door that's doubled to accommodate boxes like mine. Behind us, a man who doesn't belong gets in, but no one pays attention. The service is about to begin and I am ready.

∾

Picture number three: my children watch the man reading the lines I wrote for them. They're very surprised. I didn't tell them I could write, and they always assumed I was illiterate. They wouldn't even know I could use such a word as "illiterate." "*Mamita!*" "Who would have thought!" I can read on their foreheads. Well, little ones, I learned. Why not?

I don't visualize the reader, only the vague outline of a light-skinned man. Confirmed he's not one of us; the man is a *Gadjo.*

I can hear his voice with clarity. It makes the music of a train, which is the kind I want to hear when I'm gone. He's trying hard, like he should. From my casket I can smell his fear building up as he reads—fear that we will kidnap and steal his children, fear that we have magical powers. Fear makes him good. The man is reading for his life. Who could do a better job?

❧

Picture number four: all of my children have dressed up for the occasion. My boys got their hair gelled and neatly combed back. I can see traces of the comb, like narrow trenches ploughed on their heads. They're not light on the gel; it's tradition, something that cannot be shampooed easily. It doesn't matter that I don't like it, that I like their hair unruly and puffy on their skull. I don't get to be picky, even for my cremation. It's a package. What I have is a choice of perspective; I can open my brain to different angles of the room and outside of it. If perspective is something I can still have, then I don't mind those images.

I see their eyes darted on the white man. He stumbles on my lines; he coughs in his fist to regain confidence. They're toying with him as much as I'm toying with them. It's a *danse macabre*, and we're a people of good dancers. Everybody knows that.

Even if my vision is one I have cooked up inside my dead body, it is just as unpixelated as a live performance. I have cleaned up the time between my children and me. I have swept leftover vital space on my broom. Everything is as real as the small wrinkles on my children's foreheads. I have nailed my box and picked the crematorium. It is not too far and not too close.

❧

Picture number five: people in the city get to see the smoke. It rises to the north like the vertical contrails of an airplane. It is not me yet; I am not in it. It comes from the ever-alight hearth, the furnace temperature now gradually ascending to a boiling climax. Despite the stiffness, my body is full of water, and it will take a lot of heat to vaporize it all. In a few minutes I will shoot upward, and once again I realize that it is a one-way trip I've taken. I don't mind this actually. I am quite pleased with the rocket-launch departing. We are a traveling people, and I am no exception.

The crematorium is not far from our encampment. The *Gadjo* tells my children they will have to move once this is done. I don't want them under the sky I will occupy. I need to rest and they need to live.

A few miles away, a wanderer asks his friend who in their right mind has lit a fire in the midst of August.

Stranger: I am not in my right mind and no longer in the right body. If anything, I have earned the right to insanity, and it took me a lifetime.

෴

Picture number six: I asked the *Gadjo* to hold my hand as he addresses them. This was a sidenote to my speech, scribbled in the margin. I wasn't sure he would get it. As a matter of fact, I was quite certain he would ignore it but he doesn't. It turns out the *Gadjo* is a dutiful man. I can see clearly that he does this with no heart but a lot of guts. Try holding the hand of an unknown corpse as you read their last words, and tell me about it . . .

If I were still alive, the feel of his hand would arouse me. There is nothing more exciting than the touch of a reluctant body. No age for this. Given time and space to repent for my fornication, I repent not. I make the *Gadjo* say that, and his white skin turns bright red. An awkward silence has fallen from the ceiling, and an angel is passing through the room. I wonder whether the angel is the cause or the effect of the silence. I can never tell those things.

In any case my children are starting to have a good time; I can see Fonso's sinuous lips lifting slightly upward at the very tip. He's resisting it. *You can do it, Fonso, hang in there.* My son. In the last row Zolfina is tilting her head down and placing a rangy hand over her mouth. I could spot her miles away. And in the middle of them, Sara is holding her stomach with both hands.

Damn. I wasn't going to make them laugh—or at least not until I had thrown some good advice in their heads.

∽

Picture number seven: my baby brother just lit a cigarette. There are "no smoking" signs on every door and every wall, but Alfredo doesn't read. I wish I could smoke. I really want to roll myself one. Smoking is very high on the list of the things I miss. If I smoked now, the tip of my cigarette would make little loops in the air like it does in front of Alfredo's face. No one asks him to stop. Alfredo is not one to be stopped. He's too big and too scary for that. Asking Alfredo to stop would be like standing on the railroad tracks and putting your hands forward as the train comes.

If I hadn't forgotten to ask him in my speech, Alfredo would walk forward, disentangle my hand from the *Gadjo*'s, and give me a puff. He would whisper in his deep raspy voice: *Here you go, sister, here you go.*

Incidentally, I died from smoking. I take it as definitive proof that there is an order to all things. I had been waiting for cancer for so long, I couldn't possibly leave without it. So take me, God, but please take my tobacco along for the ride. And don't forget the paper.

God, who in the meantime has crept up next to the *Gadjo*, acknowledges. He always does. Of all things, He's pretty good at that.

∾

Picture number eight: the *Gadjo* is done with the reading. I can tell he's exhausted.

He is a man who, within the walls of a crematorium, has swayed madly upward like those inflatable figures on the side of the highway. For the first time I notice he has bushy eyebrows. I always assumed he wouldn't really have a face. He has a face after all, and one I can see clearly through the hole of time. I don't mind. It is not a bad face. Just a face with bushy eyebrows, which is now looking down at me.

They all follow his example.

They gather around the box and they lean over. Emilian lifts one of the golden coins off my eyes and checks me out. He sees my eyelids closed, perhaps for the first time. I never let them see me asleep; I kept my bedroom door locked at night. A sleeping mother is a monster.

But now they look and they can't seem to get enough of me. It is very hot in the room. It is small and crowded and not very well insulated from the furnace. My children don't mind the heat; they buzz around like flies—all trying to elbow their way up to me. I am not interested in what they see of me. I don't want to know whether the mortician did a good job.

∾

Picture number nine: I couldn't avoid that one. Along with all of them, I take a good look at myself and it's not pretty. My chin especially, it is receding. I cannot hold it in any natural way under my mouth. I don't have any holding capacity. You'd think stiffness would help but it really doesn't, quite the opposite. My chin hangs low under my face as from a broken string. In my lifetime I have been accused of many crimes but definitely not a receding chin. They could have tied a kerchief around my head as for a raging toothache but they didn't. I hate to have this closing image carved into them, the everlasting shot: *Mamita* with the floppy chin.

What's worse is the softness of tissues, the idleness. Apathy is the word; I have no passion left in my skin. I am deflated; I am a sagging woman. Perhaps I should embrace the sweetness of the void, like one accepts sleep. No matter. Acceptance of a slothful skin coat is not in me, never has. Some things never change. Please get me out of my sight.

But they won't hear me. Not after what I told them through the *Gadjo*. My words have opened hidden furrows in their skin, and they're getting all fusional on me. It's not so much what I told them. It's the mere fact that I had it in me to talk to them, that I chose a stranger to do it, that the stranger did a much better job than any of them, that I am their stranger, that I am their mother, that I am their strange mother: *Mamita extraña*.

Picture number ten: in one corner, someone called the Master of Ceremonies is trying to raise the curtain to the furnace. Only the curtain is no more than a garage door, and something is wrong with the opening mechanism. It's gripped. The screen only opens halfway. It makes funny noises. It sounds like the gurgles of a giant with really bad stomach flu. It is stuck half shut and half open. The dramatic effect is completely missed, and I am so relieved that the attention of my children has drifted away from my face.

For a few minutes it is total chaos. The MC is desperately pushing on the buttons of the panel next to the screen. Alfredo is beside him, which would drive anyone to the edge under the circumstance.

I love this moment.

My children start to unwind from their torpor; they engage in small talks across the room. This is recess. They enjoy the intermission. I am not entirely gone yet, and they have some time to kill. A facetious spirit drifts among them, and they wonder whether it is mine—a simple nontalking me who decided to linger with them a little while longer. I just had to press pause and they're free.

I can tell because they do things without thinking, things a bit unthinkable next to my dead body. Fonso picks his nose and rolls on the coarse texture between his thumbs; Sara kisses her girlfriend on the mouth; Zolfina twists Emilian's hair around her long fingers. Even the *Gadjo* makes his fingers crack and checks his nails. Alfredo puts a friendly hand on the MC's shoulder, who's about to pass out.

I love this moment.

Two technicians materialize out of nowhere, and they start working on the curtain.

∽

Unnumbered picture: they've fixed it. Two undertakers start sliding me into the hole. The MC puts on music, something classical. Taaa-taa-di-daah. Taaa-taa-di-daah. It is holy music, if holy is the adjective for full of holes. It trickles out of four speakers hidden in the ceiling. The music pours out of a machine, it is recorded and served cold; unmistakably dead like me.

At first, none of them seem to notice. It is so completely off. I have this weird feeling in my center that my children are dead too, that all of my people are dead. We're all zombies walking the surface of the earth, capable to stomach dead music for our dead; perhaps we've been dead all along, we've just lived in the pretense of life. That's a new perspective. A perspective I hate as much as the notes regurgitated from hell's studios into this room. I am already halfway into the furnace; one more push and they'll close the rickety screen on me.

Alfredo is the first to move. He goes to the MC and murmurs something into his ear. I've never seen Alfredo murmur anything to anyone. Whatever it was, his new buddy the MC makes the holy music stop.

They also make me stop on my orbit to the boiler; the undertakers stop; everything stops. No one beeps. They're all in waiting. Me too.

The first note from Emilian's violin hits us like a *banderilla*, and something inside us is starting to bleed. Yelena's haunted voice gushes straight out of her core and pours salt on our wound. Later, Zolfina's banjo tries to mend us from them both with a few stringy tricks, and she prevails for a few measures. Then Fonso's accordion takes over, and the road is in the room, not just a few yards of it that you'd believe is all that could fit in the crematorium: the whole entire thing—all the road our people ever traveled. The room is cut deep in the middle, and we are all falling. My children's music is sliding forever, and they push me onto the burner because it is time. I am burning in a room full of noises that capsize into one another.

The *Gadjo* is crying.

Forgetting

I forgot my son on the *Col des Aravis*.

This is how I recall it happened:

At one o'clock in the afternoon on August 23, 1983, six of us sit in two cars following each other on the winding road to the *Col*. In the head car, I'm driving and my father sits next to me, my window down one inch, letting in spiky surges of alpine air. My eight-year-old son lies across the seats in the back. He's sleeping; he's slept from the start. The oily green of the slopes and my son's shallow breathing has left us wordless, silent all the way, feeling solemn for no reason. Or maybe my son is not sleeping, maybe he's faking it to avoid conversation, and the two of us in the front pretend we don't know his act, respecting his childish truce, causing in each other unspoken gusts of tenderness. Looking in the rearview mirror, I can see the second car right behind us. It's close enough to see the facial expression of my mother driving, lifting one hand from the steering wheel to point her finger at the mountaintops on the left side of the road. She's in control of the vehicle and its surroundings; been there before, this is her childhood territory, now playing tour guide for us visiting family. My teenage daughter is in that car nestling her head against my prehistoric grandmother.

In the protective bubble of the car, I feel part of this lineage of Nordic dreamers, somehow stuck between generational aspirations, with enough vision to pursue scientific research and play Bach's sonatas, but lacking the boldness to ever become an astronaut or sing opera under the morning shower. I am the kind satisfied with my own shyness, never imagining the terror that will follow. A large section of my memory of that moment hinges on the rearview mirror. I look back and I look back. I see my son sleeping, my mother driving, and at the bottom of it all: I see my eyes looking.

When we get to the *Col*, we have to drive to the end of the main road to find two parking spots, one on each end of the gravel-covered lot. My father makes me maneuver until the nose of the car faces out, ready to leave. It's tricky for the spot is tight and a number of cars enter the lot at that time. I grumble and joke about my father's obsessive disorder on the subject of the art of parking; it's an old story between us, as old as my driver's license. My son is still asleep despite the commotion and the slamming of the front doors.

Then I say: Wake up, Mousse, you can't stay in the car, my love. Let's go take a look at the shops, maybe we'll find a souvenir for Daddy.

I don't remember him answering. I just see my right hand pushing the red button to unleash the seatbelt, and then his small body unwinding from his cradle position. I take his hand to extract him from the rented car.

Outside it looks like a postcard from *The Sound of Music*: the part where Julie Andrews spreads her arms open and her skirt twirls around her and the lush fields and the snow-covered blue mountains belong to her as much as she belongs to them. I take a big gulp of air and squeeze my son's hand and the three of us head down to the other car. I decide to ignore the uneasiness I always feel when stuck at the bottom of a slope. Here there's not one but two green slopes sliding toward us; it's grandiose like two oversized waves of land forming an arrowhead.

When we approach, my mother's loud, too loud for a normal conversation.

She says it's too late and at first I'm wondering what it is too late for.

My grandmother stays in the car and her window is down. She cannot get out of the car on her own and now I'm guessing that she really doesn't want to. Her face is inscrutable with a hint of violence. Or perhaps it is silent resignation, or regret, or something along the line of: It was awful, but now I've said it. She's the one to whom my mother keeps saying it's too late. Too late to apologize, that is. That much is said.

A horn blows somewhere in the parking lot. My mother breaks away from us and heads for the souvenir shops or the small chapel at the end of the road or whatever lies as far as possible from the car. I watch myself looking at my mother's back, and I'm envious of my own composure. It may be the excess of oxygen at that altitude. Or the habit of their drama.

In any case I do not know what's coming, because this is *before*.

There's no wind. The air is stagnant yet completely clear. My father makes a small hand salute and lights up a cigarette. I think I smell the smoke. I think I try to breathe it in. It makes me bend my neck. That smoke is another thing that gets me high, blurry on the edges.

It's OK, I say. Then I watch myself tapping lightly on my grandmother's shoulder and asking if she'll be fine, if she needs anything while we take a short walk. Oh, you know . . . she says, and I nod in agreement. I really do know, but I cannot put that knowledge into words. I am the sort that can only focus on one thing at a time. That one thing right now is my son's shirt. He put it on backwards. The care label is sticking out. I hadn't noticed before; I should have noticed. The way it works, or the way it's supposed to work: I notice my son's shirt, which is inside out and I correct it. Or I plan to correct it. It's the thought that counts. In a moment or so I will take my son to a public bathroom and I will have him take his shirt off and put it back on the right way, with the label scratching the skin between his shoulder blades. He will fuss and I will insist that we take care of that now because it matters to me that he looks good. He will say that I am not the boss of him and I will deprive him of that childish illusion. Oh yes, I will say, I am very much the boss of you.

In that one minute I don't think I have any doubt, I don't think I wonder whether this bossiness is something I have to put on, like a nightgown, in order not to feel naked.

And maybe I feel I can manage all the nurturing, for all of them. Maybe I don't even have to think about it. It's as natural as the warmth produced by a light bulb. Maybe I would only be flipping through a photo album now, if things weren't about to go the way they go. But in that moment in the bathroom, I make the mistake of looking at myself in the mirror. I see my mother's purple eyes in my own, her sorry-dog look that she carries with elegance. They look at me, those eyes, and they don't get it.

And I imagine my grandmother in the car picking her nose where the ingrown hair has grown—and I rush out of the bathroom, only to see my mother's back again, my mother with her raven hair and her dark blouse, making a phantasmal shadow puppet. She's hunched up like a six-year-old and I can no longer deny my own part in this play or how inadequate my slowness is as I look left and right, as I cross the road back to where she's standing near the parking lot. I will not shout, Mom, just forgive your mother's sloppiness and move on. And it's not easy not to say it. Or maybe it's easy.

At any rate she's buying something from one of the stalls, my mother. I stay behind. Perhaps ten or fifteen meters from her, I watch the snow on the ridge. I notice the passage of clouds beyond the Mont Blanc, perhaps I feel the wind rising. There's so much time there. A preposterous pack of seconds. But there's something else, too: the promise of fear, as if the air had turned solid. Only it's gone by the time my father walks up to me and asks to please take my mother with me in the car. He will drive the second car. My mother will have the cathartic talk with me. He does say *cathartic*. I see myself nodding again. The lot is packed now.

We leave fast because my car is parked right and ready to go. The first thirty-five kilometers are quiet, the inside of the car crammed with our breaths. I think I'm thankful to my mother for not talking, to my daughter in the back for reading despite the turns. My father's car is the one two cars down behind us. I see he's behind us. I see bits of his car in both wing mirrors. The bits outside my peripheral vision, in my blind spot.

Kilometer forty-two is when the beginning of a question first crosses my mind. I know because we're arriving close to Thones and the one embranchment where I don't know which way to go. There's a kilometer marker marked forty-two, white and yellow and trite. Which way do I turn? I ask. Left, my mother says. Wait, she says. We could take the old route, too; it's longer and there's a short section of highway, but it's worth it—so picturesque. Which? I say, and it sounds annoyed. Right, she says, make a right.

I make a right and after a minute or so I check whether my father's car is still behind. And it isn't. Now the doubt that surfaced at marker forty-two grows out of its own limbo. Insistent. Hitting in my head like a small hard ball on a squash tennis court. Is Mousse in the car with my father? Do I know for a fact that my son got in my father's car? Did I see Mousse in the parking lot after I left the bathroom? Did I officially ask my father to take him in? Did my father assume I would take Mousse with me? Does everyone just assume Mousse is in the other car? I see myself tightening my grip on the wheel, scratching my knee. My armpits start itching. But wait: I saw the top of his head in the mirror. I did. Him sitting in the back in the center, snug behind the two of them up front. The top of him barely making it in the reflection. Positive. A puff of my son's hair is imprinted in my short-term memory in an active and accessible way. I watch myself dismissing my instinct, thinking it's absurd. I watch myself not sharing any of this with my mother or my daughter. There is a toll ahead. We're about to enter the short section of highway. I will need the pass, which is in the glove compartment. I ask for it and my mother cries out. It makes me jump and swerve off to the emergency lane. Her hand pulls out something sticky: a half-sucked lollipop. Mousse left it there yesterday or the day before. For an instant, the red lollipop seems like another shot at salvation—because of its brightness, or the sweetness, or because it conjures my son's sugared lips. I see my mother lifting it up in the sun, and I see myself wanting to ask her and my daughter whether they saw him get in the car, or if they looked back and saw him once we were driving. Just to make sure. Then

I have to lower my window because the pass is not working and I have to pay with cash after all.

Hello. Nice day. Here's your change.

And my mother reaches over. She tries to toss the lollipop into a trashcan next to the toll booth. She misses and the red candy crashes into the pavement. After that I think I don't want to talk. I think I'm paralyzed. I have this idea that if I ask the question, it will make Mousse disappear from my father's car, where he is for sure, taking the second half of his pretend nap.

I want to get to Annecy and see them. My mother seems to have forgotten all about her altercation with her own mother. She does not have the cathartic talk. Maybe mercy is in the slowness of the scenery or in the palm of my daughter on her shoulder. When she starts speaking, I listen to her comments with only half an ear; she names each mountain, each unsigned village. She talks about family friends I don't think I've ever met. Her chatter has this anesthetic effect, the kind I loved as a child. And now I think it terrifies me, this numbing. I drive faster. I want to beat the traffic.

∽

At one o'clock in the morning, I sit in the inspector's office at the central police station. The inspector is telling me that my son's disappearance is the sort that happens all the time, with a peak in August and in the places with the most tourists. The inspector is good-looking. I see my-self encumbered by her beauty. Maybe I shouldn't look at her when she talks; maybe it would help looking at the ground. She's explaining to me what they do when a child goes missing. She's saying that the law mandates that they respond immediately, that they enter the child's informa-tion in the National Missing Children database, that they contact INTERPOL. She stops and asks if I understand. I must have said I understand because that triggers a series of questions and instructions.

She asks me to please look in all the rooms of my grand-mother's house. She asks me to please check the backyard if there is one. I keep saying I have forgotten him on the *Col des Aravis*, in the bathroom. Maybe I just imagine I say that, maybe I don't talk. She asks me where my husband is. This I tell her because she asks me to please check whether Mousse is with his father in Paris. When we're done, when I stand up to leave, when we shake hands, when she taps on my shoulder with her free hand, she says it isn't rare to find a child asleep in a hiding place or in a closet.

For the third time in twelve hours, I drive back to the *Col*. This time I'm alone. Maybe they let me go. Maybe I didn't tell them and I slipped out. I decide to stay there in the car in the parking lot next to the bathroom. At night, there's no one. It's packed with a few things that glow. The snow on the ridge glows. The bell on the chapel glows. The rented car glows when I get out of it to check the bathroom—once again—just in case. I open the door to the stall where Mousse was earlier. He isn't there. Someone hasn't flushed and the smell of urine is pungent like after eating asparagus. I get out before I get sick.

I have brought the posters with his picture, and I watch myself nailing them to the wooden lampposts, using thumbtacks. There's no hammer sound other than in my head. I look at Mousse and his missing front incisor; I touch the hole every time I move on to the next lamppost. Not a very recent photo. My husband is the one who takes all of them and he's in Paris or on the first train to Annecy.

By morning, my car is out of gas from idling, but I have one full can in the trunk. The shops reopen at nine. I question all the shopkeepers and they are supportive, even though none of them seem to recall Mousse. They say this has happened before on the *Col*. One of them gives me the number for a specialized association called Sixteen Thousand Missing Children. I try to call the association from a booth but it is Sunday and I have to leave a message. On the recording, I say I forgot my son on the *Col des Aravis*. His name is Mousse. I say I was trying to get his shirt back on the right way and then I got distracted and I left him there. I say I am on the *Col*, waiting. I try to say more but the recording doesn't take messages over one minute long and it cuts me off mid-sentence.

Later my husband and someone from the association

come to get me. They say Mousse is back at my grandmother's house. Somebody has taken him there. They
don't know who.

My husband says that when he gets there earlier that
morning, my grandmother's door is pushed open, blowing a summer wind in the hallway, the sort that rattles
around in corridors between mountains, lifting the pages of the phone book left open on the writing cabinet. He
sees Mousse there disheveled by the gusts; squatting in the
frame like a china boy and hungry for breakfast.

If I am the kind of woman to have forgotten her son in a
public bathroom, this is the sort of image I will latch on to:
the sort of recounted memory I will build for myself as if I
had been there in the hallway instead of waiting for him in
the wrong place. I will hang on to that moment precisely
because I will not have been there in it, with an embrace
that my son won't ask for—because I myself won't know
for sure whether I'm still capable of a squeeze—because
somewhere at the bottom I will carry this atrocious doubt.
And all I will have is the memory of a squeeze, the memory
of love. Not the thing itself. Not my son.

Polish Dusk

It was the day after the mine explosion in their potato field, and a lot of things hadn't changed: the forest at the end of their land was still eating itself alive, their exiled daughter was still planning to visit for Christmas, and the German Shepherd kept barking at its own echo on the other side of the valley. Their solitude was still a pet, although farmers don't have pets, but this one they had adopted, along with a perfect economy of words. They continued writing little notes to each other since they lived on somewhat different schedules. The notes said: "Need a new mop. Thank you." or "New saddle needs cleaning, saddle soap in the cupboard." The notes expressed needs related to the tasks they went on accomplishing.

What changed took the form of what they no longer did: not going to the village on the horse-drawn sleigh, not pruning the shrubs at the end of the orchard, not holding the door for the cat. The not-doing felt in tune with the absence of noise that followed the detonation. Old habits were muted or stopped: they neglected boiling their milk, their feet no longer protruded from the covers, the fore-cast of the weather in their bones was muffled or forgotten.

They, who had been the quintessential growers and raisers, had reached a state of limbo, although it didn't feel like the border to anything, or like an abode of unbaptized souls. As a matter of fact, they didn't think about their souls a lot. Amongst other things they didn't overthink or underthink. Something in them just trickled like dandelions growing wild. Their thinking had been as steady as the breathing of their horse, and now it sparked in random directions, like the flesh of the girl who had died in the bang.

A few days went by and they politely received the members of the local police force investigating the case. They offered coffee to the combat engineer in charge of mine-sweeping the four acres of their land. "*Prosche, prosche,*" they said—*go on, you're welcome*—and they encouraged all to take more cakes. Cakes made with berries and fruits from field and forest. The police were grateful and apologetic; the combat engineer had a baby face with golden eyes magnified under his visors. But to them, this decency wasn't welcome; it was heavy as a collar. They constantly expected another boom, maybe just a thud this time, in the orchard, in the barn attic, in the horse stall, and then they would be made to explain themselves. It wasn't so much the cataclysm that troubled them, but their own hope for it. They thought they would grow out of it, but nothing was growing out of this hope, certainly not carrots or wheat, only limbs of human flesh. At least the visits kept them busy picking berries and making cakes. The girl turned out to be from Belarus, a likely victim of human trafficking. So they were told.

When the police and deminer finally left, they had sat outside their porch and smoked. Eventually the sun had loosened into the lower clouds with a yellow cast, indicating that the next-day storm would come from the southwest.

∾

Along with the stormy weather came the reporter. They liked her on instinct. She was tall and lean and her eyes shifted to the side when she smiled. She was curious about them, which in and of itself was peculiar, as they didn't feel like the kind to arouse curiosity, although they understood that they were now part of a bigger story. They didn't think of it in story terms, but they were made aware of the texture of time: before the explosion and after, before the Belarus girl and after; now the police, now the reporter. It felt like being on either side of a dash on an invisible calendar; and as if in imminent justice, they couldn't find the outdated almanac in their kitchen drawer. When the reporter indicated that she would remain in the village for the night, they spontaneously offered her to stay at the farm. Przyrowa didn't have a hotel, they said, and they felt odd saying the word *hotel*. The reporter was not shy. She was at ease with her own habits of smoking and drinking black soda of which she had brought about forty cans.

Both the cigarettes and the black soda were labeled "light," which comforted them for no specific reason.

She loved their food, and they didn't dislike the black soda. They joined her after lunch to smoke on the porch, watching diagonal strips of rain. Then she asked them if they were ready, and they didn't feel ready at all, but were too intimidated to say so. She had a lot of questions, she said, but also wanted to share some of what she had found so far; it seemed fair to her to tell them a bit about who had died on their property and what had led her there. They brought some slivovitz and filled three miniature colored glasses.

The Belarusian was native of a village similar in size to Przyrowa, and her name was unpronounceable in Polish— something vaguely related to beekeeping—she would call her B to simplify. It was assumed that a childhood friend had attracted B into a prostitution ring led by two mis- leadingly handsome Serbians. Here the reporter paused to show them three photos of the said Serbians, as if to attest that she didn't exaggerate when she had said misleadingly handsome. They looked at the photos and could see how the Serbians were handsome; it was less evident to them as to how that was misleading. They courteously handed back the pictures without any comment. A few days ago in Kraków, the police had found the dead body of a politician gagged with his own underwear, and although there was no proof, the reporter strongly believed that he was B's vic- tim and that after the killing she had fled into the Polish countryside. B was barefooted, she said, as if that mattered more than anything. She drank a swig of slivovitz, and they refilled her glass. More importantly, she said. And they wondered what could now be more important than what they had heard so far. More importantly, she said again, I have found this. And she showed them a worn photo of their farm. It came from B's belongings; how the reporter got hold of it, she would explain. They felt a medley of guilt and catatonic shock. The reporter apologized. She had been too abrupt sharing this without context and understood how much of a shocker that would be. They would figure this out together, she said. But a surge of fatigue was now descending onto them; they had no idea what to say or ask. The reporter had stopped talking as if reading their mind. The photo lay on the table, unnerving. It was their farm and it wasn't. The light in it was overexposed and the colors distorted, giving the feeling that the trees and walls had been caught by surprise.

The storm brought relief by way of a window swinging wide open and the instant smell of wet pebbles and dead butterflies. The picture flew facedown on the ground, and the bottle of slivovitz was knocked down. The reporter helped to put things back in order and slid the photo in her satchel. Maybe they could take a pause, she suggested. She would go to the village and they'd restart the interview after dinner. They didn't disagree. They would take her on the carriage to the village after the rain. It was a nice path and the horse needed to loosen up his legs. They

were hospitable people, she said. In fact they didn't know
how else to be.

∾

When the rain stopped, a car parked at the end of the orchard. It was a big car—a German brand with a Spanish
name. The car made the reporter extremely nervous. She
babbled that she couldn't be seen here at the farm; did they
have a place she could hide if the people in the car decided
to come and take a look? There was a pantry adjacent to
the kitchen. Without asking questions, they locked her in
the pantry amongst the apples and the sawdust. Thank you,
they heard her say across the wall. "*Nie ma za co,*" they said
in the long Polish form—*you're welcome.*

The people in the car came and took a look; two men,
whom they recognized as the handsome Serbians from the
pictures. The first one remained silent—a fair type with
gray eyes, a split chin, and hair as thick as new grown rye-
grass. The darker one was smiling nonstop, a smile that uncovered a portion of his gum and sparked wrinkles around
the eyes. He spoke a clear although heavily accented Polish.

Had they seen a girl in the last month or so? Yes.

Did she look like that picture? The girl exploded. How
would they know what she looked like?

Exploded? There was a mine in their potato field. They
had plowed the field for years and nothing had ever happened. That girl, however, had hit it. It was incomprehen-

sible. The police and a deminer had come after that. No other mines were there. Just that one. That was that.

The silent one cursed; they didn't understand the curse, but they knew he was cursing.

No other visits? No. No other girls? No. No reporter? No. This is no place for tourists. Although it's true that counting the girl, the police, deminer, and now them, it was getting more crowded than it had ever been.

The darker one stopped smiling. We'll be back, he said. Then the Serbians left and sat in the big German car. In a car like that, one could spend a night. They didn't like that line of thought but couldn't help having it. They felt worried for the reporter in the pantry. They felt responsible. They looked for the salted caramels usually reserved for Sundays when they came back from mass.

Nothing felt right—a feeling that clearly emerged as they chewed on the caramels—wedged between the Serbians on the outside and the reporter on the inside. There was a steady increase in gravity, leaving them nailed like Jesus onto the kitchen chairs, their backs a bit hunched. Their blood flow was getting heavier, slower. It was like letting go to the bottom of a lake before a big push upward. They could go up or down. That was the problem: their sense of direction breaking loose. They hated the uncertainty and the loss of sameness. The sky had fallen onto their heads, and they didn't want to walk on clouds.

The reporter knocked on the wall. Once. They didn't respond. The reporter knocked a second time. They ignored her again. The reporter knocked louder.

Where were they? she shouted. SSSSHHHH, they said, the Serbians were still at the end of the orchard. She should stay put.

Stay put? Yes, until the Serbians were gone.

What if the Serbians stayed? She would have to wait until the night.

What time was it? They didn't know; they didn't have a clock. It must have been late afternoon according to the shadow of the walnut tree.

She was thirsty. She would have liked a soda. They told her to eat an apple instead. She said that it was pitch dark in the pantry and that she had no idea where the apples were. They said the shelves were full of apples, so it shouldn't be too hard. She was scared, not only of the Serbians. They tried to appease her. They told her the apples were real juicy and that the black soda wouldn't quench thirst anyway. They asked her whether that was the real purpose of the soda, to not quench thirst. Was that why she was traveling with so many cans? She responded that she wasn't sure. She said she had a hard time having a conversation across a wall. They understood. They asked her to be patient. The Serbians would go eventually.

But their own patience seemed to stall invisible clocks. Time was losing its parameters, and they felt they were drifting in the kitchen, although they hardly moved. It wasn't entirely bad, although it was mostly not good. A fly landed on the windowsill in slow motion. They looked at the insect washing its hands. For a while, their entire thoughts were occupied by wings and compound eyes. They started to see with the fly's mosaic vision. Through their kitchen window, thousands of tiny images coalesced into one single hallucination: the Serbians in one big German car. They sighed, which made the fly take off and get stuck onto one of the sticky ribbons hanging from the ceiling. It was getting late; they started peeling potatoes and grating sour, salted cucumbers for an *ogórkowa*.

They hadn't yet finished the soup when there was a honk. They looked up and saw the Serbians pointing their fingers at them through the open car windows. They pulled the curtains and resumed work on the soup. There was a protective sour smell around them; they wouldn't even need to add a squirt of cream. The German car roared one time and then they heard the declining sound of the Serbians driving away.

The soup was now simmering, and they let the reporter out. She was disheveled and sweaty. One of her cheeks was creased, and she looked like a dunce surprised while sleeping in class. Sawdust was on her clothes and skin. Wouldn't she want to take a bath? She could smoke in the bathroom if she wanted to. They would clean her clothes. Thank you, she said in a way that made them care. When she got out of the bathroom in a robe and a turban, she apologized.

What for? they said. For the Serbians. For the picture of the farm. For that impossible story.

They said that those things happened even if they knew that it wasn't true. Those things were not meant to happen. They asked if she still wanted to go to the village. There were another two hours until dark. Maybe she would be safer away from the farm. They could hide her in the back of the carriage. The reporter accepted.

∽

The path was black and white. The entire countryside seemed deprived of color at dusk. The reporter made a comment about that. Since she was hidden, it sounded like a voiceover in one of the movies they'd watch at the collective television in the village.

Still, it was a fine piece of land, the reporter said.

Yes it was. They had never thought of leaving their land, the place where they were born. They had felt ill, almost sick when their daughter had indicated she didn't want the family farm. A kind of prison, the daughter said, adding that there was no future in farming. They didn't think in terms of "future," which by definition was beyond them. The daughter had written a school essay about farms in Poland. The majority of which were tiny, inefficient, and unsanitary. They perpetuated poverty. They had let her go. To them their daughter was much like the cat purging and playing in the pasture. It would be hard to persuade them that the cat didn't want to be that creature that didn't want to be petted. They just couldn't keep her.

No one can keep her, the reporter said.

Who? they said.

Your daughter, no one can keep her.

Why would you say that? they asked.

We used to be friends.

They didn't respond, but they stopped the carriage. They felt that their capacity to be surprised couldn't keep up any longer.

We used to be friends, the reporter continued—still hidden in the back, her quiet voice floating around them like fog. Friends, she repeated and rested on the word like an old woman on a bench. She didn't have it in her to tell them up front. It was too bizarre. She couldn't just show up and say: I used to be your daughter's friend, and then your daughter met this girl B, who exploded on your potato field, and so I felt curious. Being curious was normal for a reporter, but that was the only normal thing there.

Your daughter met B in Krakow. Krakow was a village not much different from theirs. People got to know people. B had been the kind one would sell their soul to in return for something not so well defined. That was it, the reporter insisted. That was how their daughter had lost it. Maybe she would have done the same had she met B. They shouldn't judge their daughter or even B for that matter. No one should be a judge for those things, she added. Only the Serbians would judge, and who wanted to be Serbian?

Lost what? they asked slowly.

What do you mean? the reporter asked in return.

They meant to understand what it was that their daughter had lost; the reporter had said "lost it," but she didn't say what. What was it?

Well . . . a lot of things, friendship, sleep, perspective.

They still didn't get it.

And the picture of your farm! she said, shouting like a contestant on a national game. Maybe their daughter had not lost the picture. Maybe their daughter had given the picture to B. That was a valid conjecture.

Oh! they said.

It had lasted two months. The daughter and B would meet in hotels, pretending their daughter was a client. That must have been when the picture changed hands. The Serbians had found out. The Serbians didn't miss such things. They locked B up for a while. And then B had escaped, killed a politician, and looked for their daughter. But now, as they knew, their daughter wasn't in Krakow anymore. Their daughter had moved on, and B must have looked for the place on the picture.

When the reporter stopped talking, they didn't say anything. They loosened the reins and made their horse go again. They felt she must have been waiting for some reaction from them. They didn't want to react, and largely they didn't know how they felt. They were drained. There was a blob of emotion somewhere, but that was better left alone. It would eventually grow on its own, blossom and bear fruits. In a long time, they would pick the fruits and make memory conserves. In the years that would follow, they would digest the conserves, and new sprouts would grow out of the digested memories. They sensed that the reporter felt lonely hidden in the back of the carriage, waiting for them to say something. They felt sorry for her. They felt sorry for B and for their daughter. Mostly that's how they felt: sorry.

They took the reporter to the village. She thanked them profusely. She repeated that they were good people. Sometime she'd come back and visit, when all of this was put to rest. She apologized over and over. She wouldn't stop. Then they parted ways.

On their way back to the farm, the night had fallen, and they heard the *ooh-hu* of the eagle-owl. It was a half-moon night, and the calm was only interrupted by their horse snorting. They thought that the next day wouldn't be a bad day to prune the shrubs at the end of the orchard. When they got home, the smell in the kitchen made them hungry for the *ogórkowa*. It was an eraser smell, which made them not wonder whether any Serbians would be back, which made them not think about leftover mines and what their daughter would ask or wouldn't ask when she'd visit for Christmas.

Pisces

My mother kept her friend P. in the bathroom at night because she didn't know where else to keep her. She had taken P. in to live with us after she realized that her friend could no longer take care of herself on her own. This came after an infamous incident, which I will recount later in these pages.

I was encouraged to interact with P. because, I was told, she was very social and kind and would enjoy my company in the solitude that her condition entailed. Also, and this they didn't say in plain language, my parents believed that this interaction would alleviate the solitude thrown upon me by our recent exile to Japan (we had just moved from D.C. to Toyama). I should say here that those encouragements were completely unnecessary and even counterproductive, as by the time I was ten I never responded well to direct instructions, and in fact it took me many months to let my curiosity outgrow the natural opposition to the advice of my parents. Once my rebelliousness had expired, I started spending increasingly longer stretches of time with P. in the nocturnal quiet of our bathroom. This was no secret to anyone in the family, and my mother, who was always good with naming, soon baptized those moments my "night shifts" as if I had been promoted to a de facto nurse.

P. (for privacy's sake, I will not use her full name) had learned English from a first marriage but retained a soft turn of phrase that is so pleasingly Japanese. Out of P.'s mouth, "Actually . . ." meant "No!" and "It's unreasonable" meant "Shut up and get out of my face." I learned to understand those nuances over the length of our nightly discussions. She also taught me some rudiments of Japanese, and when I demonstrated some of them—not without pride—she'd inevitably told me, "*Jōzu desu ne*," which meant "You're good," or, more exactly, "You speak better Japanese than a tadpole." By then I knew better and humbly refused the compliment in a way that meant "You're right, I'm a little further along than a tadpole." Because of her extraordinary circumstance, the sound of her voice had gotten softer too, and at times I thought I had accidentally turned on the extra-silent bathroom fan. It's undeniable that the bubble-like quality of her voice was driving my attention in ways that no other voice could have. I had to focus no less than if I had to read the lips of a deaf mute. What I relate here is the fruit of that attentive listening, which P. would have called "being a little less distracted than a frenzied flying carp hitting a group of students during a rowing competition."

The origin of P.'s ailment is mythical. By that I mean that it is so singular, it could very well have existed only in her imagination; it could have been unreal. It is the myth-like quality of the cause that has perplexed the most learned doctors and specialists. Only a traditional healer might have accepted her telling as a possibility, but then the inevitable outcome of that acceptance would have been the further embracing of her condition. A good doctor would never have tried to cure P. I hope that among the readers of these notes, some will side with me in light of certain recent events.

P.'s story started at a tiny sushi counter tucked away in the hallways of the Tokyo metro. In P.'s recounting, the sushi place was so small and placed in such a confusing way at the intersection of multiple lines where the trains ride on different levels that it was impossible to remember exactly where it was located. As a result, even the *Edokko*—that is, those descended from at least three generations of people who had been born and raised in Tokyo—could never be sure to find the place. Because of that, the restaurant would mostly remain unknown, like a word that sticks forever to the tip of the tongue. As if to reinforce that fact, the plaque at the entrance was a fine blank piece of polished wood. P. ended up in that untraceable unnamed restaurant mainly by accident.

One day, as she was heading back from work to her condo near the Ginza, she spotted a tall white man who seemed quite lost. For a tall white man to be lost in the metro was a very common incident; what was less so was the attitude of the man. When the doors of the metro closed behind him, he stood momentarily frozen on the platform, and a deep layer of longing diffused through his face, like a moon rising behind a cliff. Now, this noticeable nostalgia, which the man wore like a newly grown skin, was extraordinarily intriguing to P.: As soon as her gaze caught it, her mind started sprouting in uncontrollable shoots; and, furthermore, her usually composed demeanor became disordered. On the spur of the moment, P. followed the man, who was now headed east toward the end of the platform.

Those were the days when the Tokyo metro was still incredibly busy, when everyone had a place to go to and come from, the underground atmosphere was buoyant with that business, and P. kept herself floating about in the human sea, careful to let herself be carried only in those currents that would propel her in the wake of the nostalgic white man.

That random chase turned out to be a spiritual pursuit; it was the only instance that I know of in which she actively and willfully participated in converging to her fate. There is simply no other way to explain why she was struck by the melancholy on the white man's face, why it made her mind wade through muddled, incomprehensible dreams, and why she obeyed her impulse to follow the man. That in the end she lost sight of him and ended up winded, down in front of the nameless sushi place, was the truly accidental part. Such is the chaos at the heart of every motion, whether acknowledged or not, celebrated or not; there is no logic to be found behind our mutation. And so it was for P. herself, in her festive hunt for the wistful white man, that she ended sitting at the counter of the nameless sushi place.

∽

Behind the counter were the *itamae* and his apprentice. Only the *itamae* silently saluted P. with a little bow as she entered the place, because the apprentice was at a stage of his apprenticeship that would probably not allow him to interact with anything beside the rice, salt, and, on good days, perhaps the rice vinegar. The counter was empty at this hour, and the *itamae* signaled for P. to take a seat in the center with a small sweeping gesture of his right hand. All the white man–hunting had made P. rather hungry and behind her regular schedule. Moreover, the disappointment at losing the man had made a small compensation, if not crucial, then at least natural.

It should be noted here that P. had always embraced a strict pescetarianism, and that therefore her diet, if it included vegetables, fruits, eggs, and dairy, excluded the flesh of any animals besides the ones taken from the sea or, in very exceptional cases, from fresh waters.

I pause here to say that it is rather strange that we commonly attribute the ethics of pescetarianism to not treating fish on the same moral level as other animals. The truth of it rests on the simple consideration of a rather basic syllogism. We eat what we appreciate and we kill what we eat. Therefore we kill what we appreciate. That one should think along opposite lines and somehow envisage the possibility of only eating what one deems *killable* is a rather harrowing line of thought (not only in that it grants a fairly incongruous authority to the eater).

Whatever we may think of this, anyone who has known P. will know she loved fish well enough to eat it and therefore to kill it. Any other interpretation of P.'s diet is a travesty of any sense of justice.

To return to the sushi place: the *itamae* had not waited for P. to place her order to start working on it. In fact, the place had no menu to speak of. What each customer ate was the result of what the *itamae* intuited in them. A close yet discreet and swift observation would soon reveal the exact size, texture, desired level of acidity, and saltiness of each morsel.

P. must have caught the *itamae*'s eye and sat at his counter "cast as bait landing at the drop of a flawless fly-fishing loop." After a few minutes, the *itamae* placed before her what can only be referred to in the cumbersomeness of our language as four pieces of sushi topped with pink roe placed on a black, four-legged tray. Like all extraordinary works of art, it eluded both its creator and its beholders. Now that each grain of rice underneath their delicate pink roof was absolutely aligned and parallel, that each alignment was facing a different cardinal direction, that each morsel comprised the exact same amount of roe and was topped with a shiso leaf cut in a golden rectangle like a dignified divine comma, that the black lacquer of the tray reflected each piece in a way that only an impossibly still tropical river would reflect the slowness of the clouds, may not individually capture the absoluteness of the dish.

It was a moment, never to be repeated, of wild, indomitable ecstasy, in which the unnamed sushi counter and all its occupants vanished into the vortex of the tray. A mysterious glitter floated into the room, only visible from the inside. It is possible that at that moment, the space that enclosed the sushi place in the depths of the Tokyo metro entered a different, parallel aquatic universe; a place in which time ticked in slow motion. P.'s hair started hovering around her shoulders as if pushed from under by some warm current; the eyes of the apprentice were watering so profusely that he seemed to be wearing organic goggles; the *itamae* stood completely still, yet it seemed that the slightest push from his toes would propel him to the height of the ceiling.

As each of the four pieces of sushi entered P.'s body through her mouth, she felt what would be best described as mild germination, not quite obvious on the roof of her palate as she masticated and popped some of the roe, but indisputably palpable in her esophagus as the tiny eggs slid down, creating a slight, liquid shudder through her digestive system.

∽

I should indicate that I spent a lot of my adolescence with P. In some ways, I can say that we were the witnesses to each other's mutations: I was transformed into an adult as she gradually morphed away from her human form. Those were our formative years. In fact, I can say that our respective transformations were at the heart of the bonds that sprang between us. I was outgrowing my childhood as P.'s was being rebuilt into a new creature, young in everything she said or did. Our paths were crossing at the exact junction where one becomes who one is (or promises to be).

That P. would undergo such a mutation so late in her life—she was forty, which seemed prehistoric to me at the time—was at once awkward and delightful; P. couldn't use much of her human experience to educate herself on what she was becoming, but I could help her out thanks to my childlike lack of bias and basic acceptance of facts. P., on the other hand, educated me in ways much weirder than my parents ever suspected.

P. never doubted that her mutation originated the day she swallowed the aforementioned sushi in the unnamed restaurant. That certitude is intriguing since the first few phases of her transformation do not seem to be a continuum that would flow from there but rather a series of discrete, seemingly unrelated events that came much later in her life—during her time at our house. I learned, however, to trust P.'s intuition over any mainstream logic. Some conditions can remain dormant and asymptomatic for years before they manifest in ways as surprising and explosive as an exponential curve.

I won't dwell over the minutiae of P.'s physical transformation. Much of it would find a better home in a medical compendium. How do lungs turn into gills? How does hair become scales?

I will say, however, that her transformation had much in common with a poster I had in my bedroom at the time. The artist, a man with an unpronounceable name, had titled it "How Boats Are Born." The first picture showed a flying fish breaking out of an eggshell, and the last one showed a sloop. There were six pictures in all, each showing a different stage of the transmutation. From that childhood series, I've kept the solid and tenacious conviction that there are six stages to every transformation, in which the first four stages can hardly be called changes. The last two phases are the ones during which everything gets played: when a wing becomes a sail and a fish abdomen hardens into a hull.

Such was the transformation of P.: six stages in all, four of which were fairly moderate and the last two much more dramatic. All of which took six years, though not evenly spread throughout that time, during which I went from ten to sixteen.

∽

The incident that drew P. into our bathroom would have seemed alarming to most people, but it wasn't to us. I shall recount it in brief here since it sheds its distinctive light on what followed years later.

It was our very first and very hot Japanese summer. The

type of summer that kicks off with ferocity like the tail of a right-wing white shark with a throbbing mouth ulcer.

P. had recently moved to Toyama from Tokyo to resume her education in a field so specialized that I don't think there is a word even in Japanese that properly designates it. My mother hadn't seen P. for years. In fact, her friendship with P. had started during a school exchange with Japan many years back. Like with all childhood's friendships across continents, their conversation had resumed at the exact point where they had left off decades before, and the two of them regularly strolled through the city in interminable and sparkling discussions.

My mother made me come along one afternoon; it was just the three of us. It was one dry and brutally hot day, with a flat kamikaze wind that felt like a blow dryer pointed straight into our faces. No one had ventured outside, and we had the streets all to ourselves. A fountain was on our way, and all three of us sat in a semicircle on its edge, letting our feet splatter gently in the lukewarm yet clear water. We heard a silence coming in the distance, a sign that the wind was abating, and it got my mother and P. quiet, as if in echo of the inward floating stillness.

Suddenly P. stood and threw herself into the water, face forward, arms and legs apart slightly bent like a skydiver's. She stayed there for a long time, with tiny bubbles floating up her sides. All the while, my mother didn't move; she just held my hand and smiled without looking at me, as if in a dream. I didn't have a doubt that all of this was perfectly normal: a grown Japanese woman looking for freshness in a city fountain; my mother smiling in the hot wind. Eventually P. emerged from the fountain water and we went home. The following day, it was decided that P. would move to our bathroom. My mother, who was a woman of dazzling shortcuts, had realized on the spot that her friend had undergone the first phase of her mutation, which temporarily made her an inverted mammal. If P. had needed water to breathe, P. would always need more, and my family would provide.

Over the next few years, I bonded with P. at night and during the day we had a continuous parade of specialists visit P. to measure the growth of her scales or the increasing protuberance of her eyeballs. Each doctor was sworn to secrecy before being allowed into the bathroom, and as far as I know, they all kept their promise. I don't believe my parents had those doctors come in to really cure P. In fact, I am certain they contemplated some secret hope that one of them would fall for her, as P.'s transformation made her stunningly beautiful. Initially, the scales growing behind her ears looked drawn: like a miniature koi fish tattoo, one that would never sag as the skin grew older and less supple. Over time (as measured in years), each tiny scale acquired its own depth, like a chiseled bronze bas relief adorning the canvas of what remained of her human skin. This was an invitation to look closer, again and again, to get lost in that observation, to enter a place of prehistory where all creatures were sea creatures, where all belonged to a gigantic womb, and above that womb the earth had not a single blade of grass to offer. I wasn't exempt from the fascination that P. exerted. But I was a little girl and then a less little girl, and all the while P. allowed me to touch her scales and her budding fins. P. was my friend and my pet. She grew on me the way animals do, but with a lot more vocabulary.

Very little in P.'s behavior revealed the inevitable turmoil that raged inside her as the result of her transformation. She was very Japanese that way, repressing the flow of wrath and fear in the depth of our family *ofuro*, soaking it up in a literal way.

For the sake of clarity, I should indicate here that our bathroom was endowed with a short but deep and steep-sided wooden tub made of *hinoki*—one of those rare specimens nowadays replaced with a plastic or stainless steel equivalent. The *ofuro* had become P.'s home inside our house, and within the confines of the *ofuro*'s square walls, she held on to humbleness and emotional suppression to promote better relationships with us, and above all with me.

I now realize how deeply she influenced me that way, how much I take after her. And so I find it particularly arduous to write what comes next. The telling of these events is so heavy, just like the events themselves. I find that my admission doesn't alleviate the weight of the facts, but rather deprives me of a morsel of myself. I find myself to be my own necessary cannibal. In the end, I will write this because I have no choice: some accounts work like a school of sardines magnetically pulled toward an orca's mouth.

On the eve of my sixteenth birthday one February night, I decided to pay a visit to the bathroom. I hadn't seen P. since the night before, and even if her presence in such a strategic part of the house as our only bathroom made her uneasily forgettable, the hours passed away from P. transformed the idea of her into a dreamlike recollection. Not seeing P. (even for a little while) always raised in me a bizarre uncertainty as to the possibility of her existence. I had to go and check.

When I entered the bathroom, my irrational doubts seemed confirmed, as I couldn't see P.'s head protruding from the edge of the *ofuro* as it usually did. In a moment of panic, I rushed closer and slipped on the wet floor, landing headfirst on the *ofuro*. I lost consciousness.

When I awoke, I was still lying with my head against the *ofuro*, some blood dripping onto the dark gray tiles. I heard something that sounded like a chime, which I first attributed to my fall. When the sound didn't subside even as I shook my head left and right and yawned to unblock the pressure in my ears, I realized that it was P. calling for me on the other side of the *ofuro* wall. I sat upright and turned to peer from above the ledge into the tub.

P. was fully immersed and looking at me wide-eyed through the water. She was a little too tall for the length of the *ofuro* and had to curve her frame to allow every part of her to be underwater. Since the night before, a radical transformation had taken place. Her arms (long since covered in scales) had fused along her torso, and her feet and toes had merged into a small crescent moon–shaped tail. I understood that P. could no longer get out of the water. She couldn't talk to me. She could, however, make the chime-like sound I had first heard as I regained consciousness, a sound that was somehow perfectly understandable, like a language learned overnight in a state of intense fever.

P. asked me if I was okay. She was worried about the blood above my eyebrow, which kept dripping and falling into the water around her. I told her that I was fine, that the head was the part of the human body that bled the most. She thanked me for reminding her of that fact. She bowed her head a little. I bowed back. We smiled at each other because everything was suddenly too sad to make laughing possible.

She asked me if I knew what was going to happen. I responded that I was very, very stupid but that even a sea cucumber could feel the change in undersea weather. P. bowed again and so did I. It was getting hard on us. Neither of us was used to getting too emotional in each other's presence. I believe my eyes were starting to water, and of course I couldn't tell for her: there is no telling for those things on a fish.

It started to snow and some snowflakes hovered inside though the narrow crack of the open bathroom window. P. asked me if I could undo my hair and let the tips flow into the water. She said she missed her hair the most, that it might be the only thing she missed at all from her human form. I untied my hair and turned my face away, then draped my neck over the narrow edge of the tub and let my hair flow into the water. Nothing else happened for a while. And then I had formication, a sensation of micro-animals kneading the tips of my hair, some forever numbed nerves awakening there too. This was nice; I didn't want it to stop. Actually, I pushed my head further to let more hair into the tub.

After a while (maybe an hour or two), one snowflake fell on my nose and made me sneeze. I sat back up and turned back to look at P. She was sleeping peacefully, her quiet dark eyes still wide open. The water around her was a bit pink from my blood. One hair was floating on the side.

Looking at P. sleeping, I felt an immense and immediate fatigue, a force almost as potent as a strong anesthetic. I left the bathroom in a daze. I did not notice that I inadvertently locked the door on the inside before I got out. I did not remember falling onto my bed with my hair wet and my face bloody.

In the early morning darkness before dawn, I heard my mother shouting. It took me a minute to understand that she was calling out to her friend through the locked bathroom door. I stood and joined her. She gave me one look of utter, unbearable distress, as if pleading with me; then she destroyed the door in three pushes of her resolute body. P. was in the same position I had left her in the night before: lying open-eyed at the bottom of the bathtub water. For the next half hour, as our whole family knelt by her, it was impossible to tell whether she was alive. We all held our breath, as much out of fear as out of a certain wish to commune with her in the absence of breathing. And there, after a long stretch of anxious waiting, I had the strange thought that I was the only one seeing her tail flicker.

My mother was the first one to emerge from the collective torpor. She left the bathroom and came back minutes later with a tool box. She set out to detach the *ofuro* from the wall and from the floor, which wasn't a minor enterprise since it entailed cutting off plumbing pipes and unsealing some of the floor tiles. Then there was the issue of mobility, water being a dense element and a filled *ofuro* being well beyond the capacity of the most motivated water carriers. We set out to rework the *ofuro* into a pushcart of sorts by affixing several of my old bikes' training wheels, which had been miraculously kept through time. All of it was a formidable task and lasted through most of the day.

The sea was too far from the house for us to walk there. We had to take the train, and the walk to the station lasted two hours. We had covered the *ofuro* with its thin wooden lid, and at the last moment I had also thrown on a polka-dotted blanket from my bedroom. An emaciated station attendant escorted us to board the train with a portable ramp and called ahead to our destination station so that another emaciated attendant would be waiting for us at the other end (and he was). Even though the train was nearly empty in the late winter dusk, we must have left a strange impression as we sat on either side of the oversized container, which was making odd splashing sounds. Yet no one asked any questions. I remember one older man with white hair and a beard sitting across from me, smiling solely with the warmth of his eyes.

It was dark when we walked from the empty station to the deserted seashore. As we reached the beach, we continued pushing forward onto the sand and into the ice-cold water; we only stopped slightly past waist level, where the *ofuro* would fit entirely under the water.

We waited there in the cold Japan Sea. My mother pulled out the blanket and the slats that covered P. And it was right there, for those long minutes in the salt water, as we were yearning for P. to swim out of the *ofuro*, that the blue firefly squids started to surround us. Hundreds of them suddenly emerged out of the depths into a living belt of blue light glowing around us; the sight of them was so stunning and unexpected that for a moment our eyes veered away from the *ofuro*. That's when P. vanished, leaving no trace, not even the slightest quake of undercurrent that I would have expected to feel against my hips. From one moment to the next, the *ofuro* was empty.

It was too dark for me to tell whether my mother was happy. Perhaps there was no telling her feelings. Yet I also know exactly how she felt. I know this because I had witnessed that moments like this are subject to a certain condensation, as if the tip of our fingers felt the liquid embossing of space. P. had taught me a Japanese word that characterized this: "*mono no aware*" which can be imprecisely translated as "a gentle sense of sadness about the passing of all things."

The trip home was incredibly fast. After we dried off, my mother made matcha tea, which I drank from her bowl when she passed it to me after she had drunk first and wiped the rim clean. This was her silent way of honoring P. and wishing me a happy birthday. After which she passed a gentle finger along my bloodied eyebrow and went for a Band-Aid.

Then nothing else. But perhaps related to this is a recent strange report by the local press of a tall white man swimming along Tomaya Bay and followed by a huge, shimmering fish (not a dolphin, though it swam like one, but onlookers clearly noticed scales). A crowd gathered to watch the oblivious swimmer and his follower. The report says that at some point the human-sized fish jumped over the swimmer, who still didn't notice, and then that was it.

Legionnaire

Everything begins with the lovemaking: the coming in and the opening up, the out and the in; moment after moment, yourself grasping and grasped, seeking and sought, moaning and moaned, open-shut, over-over, lust and found; minute after minute, until it is now, this moment, the moment of your coming, the last moment, the saddest and most glorious. It is because we dream, and I dreamt myself a morning among dead mornings—now full of light because of the dream, walking up the large avenue, people coming in all directions on the sidewalk, brushing by me, the smallest emigrant, out and about, smelling new air.

First, she was a student. It was because it was the logical thing to do for girls, for her especially, since she knew nothing yet, nothing useful. She used to sit on the benches with all the others, hundreds of them. Sometimes she would forget her purpose and she would sit there, a long time after the class was over, in the empty auditorium. She somehow got the idea that she belonged to big, empty spaces, and she started looking for them. Dawn was the best time of day; the foreign city still imbued with sleep, no one there. She sat in empty train station hallways, in empty churches and temples, on benches along the river, on empty boulevards, on the roof of the opera. She sat to see the bubbly yawning before the coming of life, scraps of oily papers, torn pages of magazines, red-eyed pigeons, dog shit; she watched and smelled until she became dizzy with the surge, the spitting image of herself spat right back to her cheek. It was filthy and magnificent. Some days she wouldn't shower because she wanted the filth to stick to her skin, to become her crust. She fancied herself the heroine of a fairy tale, fleeing a lustful father: donkeyskin. She fancied herself obeying some dark fairy who would blow dust on her hair and make her vanish; and in the foreign city, she would disappear. She would be forgotten like a baby with no nametag; and no one knew her, no one at all, and it was good.

In the spring it would be warm and rainy, and her body would covet the juices of beets and strawberries. On her way to class, she could feel the ancient chestnut trees swelling with their sap, outpouring tiny buds of green. Spring was the season for people, women in butterfly sleeves and men with white shirts and pointy shoes; people would wander like bees, and she would be part of the hive, going from place to place with a reason, a function, an intent. She would get lost in the crowd, and then she'd hit a street sign—blue—all signs were blue, and she'd find her way: back to her place, to her room, the tiniest room on earth, where she had to put her shoes under her bed and her clothes in the window frame and herself on the bed. And it all fit.

Once she saw him on the square with the fountain, walking in the opposite direction—the sun hitting his forehead and light splashing into his hair. He was fast but she caught the giant eyes and the tattoo on his neck: "never seen, never taken." Why? she thought. I saw you. I saw you on the square with the fountain. I saw you in the foreign city where no one sees and no one smells. And later she thought of how fast he had crossed the square and how long she had stood there, waiting for the smell to fade. And what sort of smell was this? She had thought the foreign city had exhausted smells for her but this was new. And she waited and waited, and she tried to think and only when the smell subsided did she know for sure that the man smelled of warm sand. That spring she didn't get to see him again.

In the summer she came back to her homeland for a visit, and she became inhabited by hatred. Hatred for her father for not being lustful, hatred for her mother for being dull as the aquarelles in the kitchen, hatred for her brother for being; and being had become a sin. Home was wrong, always had been. There were no words to articulate her hatred: she drooled it, perspired it, ate it, and vomited. She strolled with them along the northern shores where beaches were covered in gray pebbles and it made her seasick. They were worried because they didn't know. And what did they know? And what was bigger than their ignorance? Even the dog didn't know, her dog, the one who had watched her from day zero, the one she had taken for countless walks and countless pees. And she tried; she tried to go and take the dog for a walk and for a pee and far into the woods and across the hedges. She watched her dog tilting his head to the side and she couldn't—she couldn't pet him. She tied his leash to a branch and she left. She took a night train back to the foreign city, and the sound of metal wheels on metal railing jumpstarted her heart again and she could sleep.

The foreign city had not waited for her. Her tiny room had suffered leaks from the roof, and the walls were covered with yellow veins and, for the most part, it didn't matter. She pretended the veins were tiny rivers, and from her bed, she'd stretch her legs and reach out and walk between them, leaving feet marks and the rivers and her feet marks she called banana trees, although she'd never seen a banana tree. Outside, a war was about to end and most were sulking; she could tell by the way they held their head slightly tilted to the side like her dog. It had been a distant war, not even covered by the headlines, not even called a war; a conflict featured right before the obituaries, a soon-to-be-dead conflict. Nothing to brag about, although it had lasted eight years. Think of it, she had been a child when it had started, happy in her homeland and all, a good daughter with a clear future. In the distant and sunny country that some had called their own, they had meant to restore order, and order had bitten them right back where it hurt most. She could have told them, for those were the sort of things she started to know; maybe she had a future in politics, maybe the general would consult her and maybe not. She couldn't go on as a student; she wouldn't know what to study anymore, her appetite for knowledge so big, it filled her before even starting a meal. An appetite like that demanded failure, and she tried selling foreign newspapers on the street. She erred in a miserable attempt to replicate *Breathless*—like in no breath—and she could tell that the times had exhausted the air and that some renewal was vital, like in life. She couldn't shout the news because nothing was new, not even her, and nothing had started yet and nothing was ending, not even a war. And so she waitressed.

The café stood at the end of her street in a parallel universe; the owner had a compulsive taste for red, and getting in was like plunging into flesh, which she took very much to heart as a dive into herself and into others. Waitressing made her talk, a talk heavily tainted by her homeland accent. She talked nonstop with no regard as to whether patrons wanted to listen, and for the most part, they wanted to, and they listened to the young foreigner with a rushed eloquence as if she made them discover their own vernacular, as if she was talking sense into them through the discovery of their language, as if she was pushing their words down their throats, stuffing them like geese. She talked about her homeland and how it was mostly black and white and how even the sea was gray. She talked about her dog and how she had left him one day tied to a tree because she couldn't pet him. She talked about the empty au-

ditorium after class and how it echoed her own breathing.
She talked about the banana trees on her walls and how
they replenished her oxygen at night. She talked about the
pigeon that laid eggs on the pot outside her window and
how it cooed with every high noon moon. And when they
asked her what she meant by high noon moon, she said
that she would ask the pigeon next time. And she became a
neighborhood celebrity. She thought she had it all figured
out because spoken words made her feel real and not in a
dream full of light where she would end one day.

And then she saw him for the second time. There he was,
in the café, smoking at the bar. She would stare at the smoke
as if it was his gospel escaping from the lips and through the
nose, and who says it wasn't? And who says the truth doesn't
reside in the lungs, at the very bottom? Why not?

From the burning tip of his cigarette, she felt a sudden
ambition for becoming an ashtray or a flowerpot or a sidewalk. And she hated her guts for being a waitress and not a
bartender. Then she just sat next to him at the bar, and she
dropped her apron on the sawdust-covered floor and felt
sorry for the apron, but it was too late. She didn't want to
talk because she was scared it would make him smile. He
ordered a drink for her, and she drank quickly because it
was pungent, because there was no time to waste on drinks,
because it was too late. He was slim and handsome and
smelled of warm sand. That's it? Slim? Handsome? That's
all? But that was all that she could come up with: slim,
handsome, warm sand.

When he undressed, her vocabulary shrunk even farther, with the exception of the tattoos that he had all over, and most were words: the neck one—quizzical: "never seen, never taken." Why? She thought. I will take you among the banana trees, and she realized that he must have been a warrior or a fighter or a mercenary, but it was too late. On his right arm, one word: "think," and this was negative knowledge for she had reached a shore, where thinking was forbidden and where feelings grew up like vines until they covered the ceiling and the window frame and under the bed where she hid her shoes. Over his chest, it read "no one," and she felt reassured because that was her, and she felt there was no possible mistake and no confusion at all, and all was logic. She still couldn't let go of the logic, but she could let go of her body.

And she let go of her skin as she ate his, full of salt beneath the tattoos. And the salt she had expected in this ocean of a man and please, please, she would love him well-seasoned. She let go of her vision as she drowned into his—his giant eyes, shiny wells of nothingness where she would read nothing, absolutely nothing. And with the thrill, the Legionnaire's eyes flashed some bright sparks like a thunderstorm sky, and she wished for the rain to come. She wished without knowing her wish because she had stopped knowing, she had stopped wishing, and she had stopped breathing. Stop, stop. But always she returned to the place inside them, back again to the place of their pleasure, their lips, their waves, their juices, back again to the corners of dark secrecy, to their in, to their out, back again to the movement of their hips, to the motion of her bed, and to the bending of their banana legs. And in the final arch, she heard it without a doubt: the bark. Muffled at first and then louder, louder, until it exploded in their ears like a hand grenade. And at this moment—at this minute—she knew that if she'd open her door, her dog would be there, his head slightly tilted to the side. But she didn't open the door, there was nothing left to say, and they didn't talk; they slept the sleep of the dead under a leaden sky, but this lead was blazing and not dull.

And in the morning he left. And he didn't say where he was going and why would he? And she didn't wait for him and why would she? She walked the streets of the foreign city, and she did what I know she knew best: smelled new air. The rain had fallen and erased every smell, just leaving behind thin watermarks.

And she made herself a life in the foreign city because that was expected of her and she expected me to. Me too, me too, one day I had expectations when I was she and she was me and not just a dream full of light.

And so she met a man, and she loved again and the man loved her back, and they had children and a dog. Someday their children would have children and a dog.

Still, because we dream, I had a dream not long ago that the Legionnaire had been found lying in the desert with his giant eyes wide open. Just like that. Just like that. Clouds were passing in the sky, and he was showing off his tattoos. Smiling, he said, pointing to his neck: "never seen, never taken," pointing to his heart: "no one." And I know he didn't know, and I could forgive him. Yes, I could. Why not? And I could help the men bury him in the desert, and I would shovel the warm sand over his face, and slowly, his smell would vanish. Just like that.

So easy.

But it isn't. Because let's face it: The light inside me only comes with the dream, and if there's a sun, the only sun is in that dream. And some nights, lust for his skin bites me like extreme cold bites fingertips. And then I need to get out. Get out! Now! And it all happens fast, and I keep forgetting my gloves, and my hands are so naked. And I walk my dog and my dog walks me. And we try, we try—each of us at one end of the leash. And we howl at the moon, and we're such big losers, but we lose in unison. And always we come back to the same place: a playground with a sandbox and my dog invariably pees in it, and I bury my feet in there, and we know that six feet under lies a Legionnaire.

Swallowing Carolyn

Lulu is late for lunch and drives a maroon wagon in a part of LA she doesn't know well. The car has a stick shift; she keeps changing gears to adjust to the traffic flow. As part of the amenities, a GPS device is sucked up firmly onto the windshield, and the GPS lady keeps shouting to bear left, to turn left, to stay in the left lane; she tries to follow directions but eventually cannot keep up with all that left and makes a right. The GPS lady seems unabashed by this and claims that they have reached their destination and indicates their total driving time. That's fine, she thinks, fine to know how long you've been driving, fine to know you've reached your destination. She thanks the GPS lady silently and turns her off.

That's fine, she thinks once more; but as she steps out of the car, she notices that the buildings on the street are in motion. Earthquake, she thinks, although the doors to the buildings are in motion too—a motion quite incompatible with an earthquake wave. The door to the restaurant, for example, keeps changing size. One minute it looks humongous like the threshold to a pyramid, and the next it looks tiny as a rat hole. She wonders whether she will fit through the door, whether she will go in at the right time—a time when the door will be large enough to frame her body and not so big that she will get lost in it. Arrhythmia, she tells herself, objects around her expand and contract like a muscle in sync with the one inside her. That's all there is, she assumes. She will ride the motion; she will fit through the door, and the red, slimy thing inside her will stop puffing.

She has to lean her whole body against the glass door to make it in, and, indeed, she fits through it.

Inside, the restaurant is long as a tunnel, and tables are placed in one single open-ended row. The place looks like the infinite reflection of two mirrors facing each other. She smiles a big smile with lots of teeth.

The four of them are sitting at the first table and turn their heads toward her at once. Carolyn's husband and her three sisters. Like in a Chekhovian play. They hug her and she hugs them back, surprised at her own strength. She presses them hard onto her chest, even the husband; she closes her eyes and closes her fists. They have had appetizers already, and their wineglasses are full.

The waitress brings in an extra chair for her, and she sits at the end of the table; a place that is not meant to be since it is blocking the way. That's the only place there is, she tells herself. The waitress comes back and fills a fresh glass with an expensive red wine. She hasn't checked the label, but she can tell the wine is expensive just from its onionskin color. She fills her mouth with it and lets it drip deep inside her throat. It makes noises on the way down, but the noises are covered by the wind inside the restaurant. The wind keeps blowing through the entry door as people come in or go out. It is funneled through the narrowness of the place in a Venturi effect. It is Carolyn's wind. A wind that messes with their hair and their napkins. The husband has no hair, and yet the wind finds ways to mess with him too, through his eyebrows or his lashes, the wind inserts itself into creases and membranes. Carolyn, she thinks.

She won't talk much; she is intent on listening. She will listen to what they have to say, especially the husband. She is also keen on watching them interact: the sisters and the husband. She has much to observe and much to learn. An awful lot for just one lunch but she does not set the rules. The rules set themselves. At first, she lets herself spin through their small talk. She learns about upcoming trips to New Zealand, about property purchase projects, about baby-making projects, about layoff risks, about interior design and medical billing rates, about urban safety, and, yes, also about the ocean temperature. It is easy to listen, and it is equally easy to shut off and go blank inside. And she keeps swinging from open to shut with the help of the onionskin wine. For a while she observes the tangible flow of their numbing appetites: appetite for food, for holding conversation, for holding a fork and a knife, for smelling wine, and for resting elbows onto the table, for crossing legs and uncrossing them, for smiling vaguely and elegantly, for asking questions, and for not waiting for answers.

Such close yet loose observation makes her slightly sick,

like someone reading the paper in a moving car. She feels the tightness of the tissue around her stomach and realizes how extremely hungry she is when the waitress drops a menu right in front of her. She has not actually seen the waitress drop it; what she has seen is the thick-folded ivory page descending slowly onto her napkin. The menu is animated like a floating snowflake.

While she waits for the slow motion descent to come to an end, she also notices the silence. A silence so abrupt, it has fallen onto them like darkness at the flip of a switch. The husband and the three sisters keep on talking, but they speak without making any noise, just moving their lips; even the silverware is turned off as it tinkles or scrapes against the plates. She yawns widely down her sleeve to pop her ears. It works for the most part, although she knows that the volume is now down a bit. Carolyn is helping me focus, she tells herself, mute what's unessential. She tries not to laugh hysterically with her dead friend and starts reading the menu.

It is a du jour menu, which means that the cook and his team must reprint it every day. Maybe they just change the date and keep the rest. Maybe the cook wakes up at dawn and walks to the market for only the freshest ingredients and then builds his cuisine around them. Maybe everyone is doing this—building their life around the freshest events. She can see that. Yet three years after the accident, Carolyn's death is to her as fresh as this morning's tomato.

Carolyn was petite and made a grand exit. She thinks

how small people take up so much room, overcompensating for their size. The coast guards never found her body, and maybe that is one of the secrets to Carolyn's freshness, her inability to rot, the pervasive expectation that she will pop out on some exotic island, wearing a straw skirt and a hibiscus necklace. Lost at sea, just lost.

She has to skip the appetizer in order to catch up with them, and the menu offers a limited number of entrees: a Colorado rack of lamb (huge and sacrificial), a traditional coq au vin (drowned in Burgundy), pan-seared day boat scallops (...), and a roasted halibut. It is an easy choice, almost a nonchoice: it is the halibut. She nearly shouts it to the waitress as she comes near. This makes Carolyn's youngest sister turn to her suddenly and ask: "Are you okay?"

Simple things are hard to explain, she thinks. She does not answer and just offers a bashful smile that is immediately returned by another smile: this one, affectionate and honest.

The youngest sister's smile provokes an uncontrolled flood of sadness in her; like often when she relaxes, when she is offered shelter or warmth, when strength or restraint are no longer needed, she feels ruptured like a dam. *Almost.* You can resist if you want to, she tells herself. Grief, much like jet lag, comes in waves, but she has long learned to ride them. Her eyes stay dry like a desert.

She remembers how those waves were merciless in the year that followed the accident. Carolyn's absence everywhere—from her kitchen cabinets to the glove compartment of her car, from the chirp of her cell phone to the burgeoning holes in her socks. Carolyn wouldn't let go. Just let go, she begged. But no, she wouldn't. Days of Carolyn's underwater hair tangled around her, and all she could do was gasp in the hope that her friend would let her resurface at some point.

When she finally reemerges from her thought bubble, Lulu needs to go to the bathroom. She asks for directions and Carolyn's second sister points to a door at the very end of the restaurant. She is surprised at her own confidence in standing up and heading that way, her legs not even numbed from being crossed awhile. She feels ridiculous pride for it. She realizes how she isn't walking but rather gliding to the bathroom, surfing on the husband's suspended gaze along her back.

Once locked behind doors, she absentmindedly watches herself in the mirror. She notices a woman and that takes her slightly aback. She has never thought of herself in womanly terms, and there in the mirror is the clear image of a female specimen with long lashes and high cheekbones. Carolyn had once joked that she didn't think of her as a man or a woman friend; she thought of her as a "neutral" friend. Now she wonders whether Carolyn had really meant "neutered," and that makes her smile. This day and around one thousand days into Carolyn's engulfment, she is finally shedding her "neutral" skin and taking a gender side. She understands this to be one of Carolyn's gifts. Carolyn had always been bighearted, but her death had been the most unbearably generous act of all. Lulu sits on the toilet and goes about her business. She remembers the many times she has peed with Carolyn in the same bathroom, Carolyn curling her lashes or plucking her eyebrows. Their intimacy had been open and simple.

As she comes back to the table, she focuses on the husband, a man once passionately loved by Carolyn. Inexplicably (another simple thing). In fact, it is the first time Lulu is seeing him after the accident. It is also the first time she attends the memorial lunch. She has been invited each and every year, but she couldn't bear the thought before and gave excuses. Lately, her emotions have worn into a more accepting condition. A condition she doesn't know whether to embrace or to hate, but a condition, after all, that has made her come to LA and rent a car and fit adequately through the glass door of the restaurant.

The husband is laughing, showing off the big gap between his two top front teeth. She knows Carolyn revered that gap; she wonders whether he smiled at Carolyn during their terrible crossing, whether her friend took with her the image of that hole, that opening of his, that display of innocence in her faulty captain. That he killed her is beyond question (and who is asking?). That he now pursues a life without her is also beyond question (so why ask?). She knows, however, that Carolyn wants her to watch, to smile at that man still embalmed in her nagging passion. Lulu wonders whether one day she will reach through the hole, whether one day the two of them will talk. She never talked to Carolyn's husband, even before her death, never really. He raises his glass and cheers with her and then cheers with the three sisters, one by one. No one names what they are cheering to, and they drink the wine with their eyes interlocked among them. The cheering lights up Lulu's memory exit sign again.

She checks out of the now and pictures herself two weeks before the crossing in a Manhattan bar with her friend. The two of them clink their glasses, and their smiles cross as in multiple handshakes. Carolyn keeps saying a journey will do her good, even (especially?) with the husband. There's a lot of food. Carolyn has ordered small plates, too many of them—she is never too tired for food, experimenting with a continual growth spurt that doesn't deliver. Carolyn has the body of an eight-year-old on stilettos.

Now Lulu tries and fails to fully capture Carolyn's silhouette. She thinks of how one never knows when they see someone for the last time and how one obsessively gropes for those moments like for car keys in a room full of darkness. She can see how last times are inevitably half-lived and how the memory of those times is unfinished. Lulu's brain catches Carolyn raising a toast between gulps of seawater.

She takes another sip of the silken wine and feels a blow in her right calf, which makes her let out an "Ouch!" It isn't Carolyn this time, and she mentally blames the flirtatious husband.

It is not the husband though, but the oldest of Carolyn's sisters. The sister apologizes and becomes momentarily bright red. Lulu thinks red is the color of happiness, and she intensely wants the sister to lock the color in her skin and stay red forever.

She doesn't know that sister very well, but she has always sensed her as a cool, calm, and collected being, and, indeed, it takes but a minute for her to get back to her typical composure. Lulu watches her being so smooth and so poised again, and she wonders where she hides all the suffering. She imagines how the suffering is collected inside the sister, like rain in the basin of a cloister's garden.

The same sister is asking the husband a question. They are talking as if in a parlor, and it hurts her to watch them. She forces herself to hold her gaze longer, but all she can see is a burned disc as if looking directly at a bright light. She winks once or twice, but the disc is still there, like a stubborn eclipse. Whether the brightness between them is genuine or affected is irrelevant; it is not their light: it is Carolyn's.

∿

She rubs her eyes impotently. Carolyn was family and now she is blocking her from them—like she does not belong, sitting her at the end of the table and blinding her with all the light. She asks her friend to please just let her sit and watch, but she won't.

∿

The invisible waitress brings her plate at last. It is a big, round plate and right in the center is the halibut on a bed of lentils. It is rectangular and slightly roasted and slightly alive. It is half and half. Not fully roasted and somewhat alive. Not alive in the sense that it can swim from the plate. Alive in the sense that it breathes gently, regularly, and very clearly. The flesh is so white, it borders on transparent. Lines on the flesh are bent, like biblical arches, holding the air above them, flutters of steam escaping at the top.

The fish has lost its eyes, and now the eyes swim underneath it. Either they have migrated out of it, or they have been pulled out of its sockets by the chef's knife. She knows that, either way, the fish has not fought. The fish has let go, and now the lentils are watching her, demanding explanations. She watches the crowd of eyes on her and feels a little nauseated. She feels hungry too.

She starts with the lentils, like a child, keeping the best for last. She pops them individually between her tongue and her palate. Long time, no sea. It lasts forever. She cannot swallow right. Some of the seeds are not quite pureed, get stuck midway, and she has to wash them down with liquids. Sisters and husband watch her pretending not to notice. She is talking to them throughout the process, now strangely animated and warm, practically bubbly.

The halibut is nearly cold when she takes the first bite.

Eat it, she hears, this is my body. She takes another bite followed by another.

At one point she looks up from her plate and asks if anyone wants to try some.

Wednesdays of the Japanese Wave

head of Wednesday . . .

In the apartment with double exposure there is, well, double exposure.

To the north, the tip of an ochre convent tower rings hourly and half-hourly. The nuns have a damper device on, and the clock sounds liquid at night.

I don't hear it during the day, which is normal because I am not here in the apartment.

To the south, the lake and the mountains are laid out in postal card format.

In July, there is a water-firework.

I don't live here in the apartment, it seems. On Wednesday, I visit.

. . . she has troubling thoughts . . .

Far, far away, there was a dog waiting at the end of the day. He barked once and I petted him on the head, then forgot his presence as I read Buzzati in the toilet.

The dog was on the other side of the toilet door waiting, not reading any stories.

There was a picture of the dog in the toilet, but I was so entrenched in Buzzati, I must have overlooked it.

When I opened the toilet door, I pinched the dog's tail. It didn't hurt him. Nothing would hurt him.

The dog was dead.

. . . and images of liberating deaths . . .

I don't mind a spider on the ceiling. Back in the nineteenth century, Parisian prostitutes used the expression as a metaphor. The ceiling being the cranium, wherein resides the spider, an animal that lives in neglected environments, thereby evoking decay. So a spider in a cranium means someone a bit deranged. Usually it is just someone eccentric who doesn't disturb others.

Under the first scenario, I pick up a glass and a piece of thick paper. I climb up a chair and enclose the spider into the glass. I slide the thick paper underneath, making sure I don't snap off one of her legs. I hold the paper firmly onto the glass and bring it outside. I empty the glass into a flowerpot, because I figure the spider may like plants.

Under the second scenario, I smash the spider with a book and dump it in the trash.

. . . as well as lucid insight . . .

Legs must be held vertically up the wall so that the blood flows down. Feet perpendicular. Arms out.

A simple pose that rejuvenates the lower back and legs, eases tension. It's been awhile since I saw you do that.

"Hold it," I say and it doesn't feel rejuvenating.

It feels like ninety-six to me. It feels like the opposite of love.

. . . into the sentence . . .

"So you will see your parents soon?"

"Yes, but not until the end of the month. There is no holiday until then."

"There is this woman in the apartment next door and she has ten children. She has a lot of visitors. When it's not a son, it's one of her daughters."

"Nice! That must be entertaining."

"What?"

"That must bring some action into the building, some fun."

"Yes. One of her sons has a relative who knew Gerard."

"That's good. So you talked about him?"

"What?"

"I asked if you talked about Gerard with the lady's son."

"Yes. How are your sons?"

"They're good. Thank you. School started last week again. Some getting used to for the small one."

"Kiss them for me, will you?"

"I will."

"So you will see your parents soon?"

. . . cast upon the woman she knows as her grandmother.

His wife, he called you.

My wife, he said, as you were right in front of him, holding a conversation with somebody else.

It didn't bother you. You never called him my husband, always Gerard. You gave him a name out of love.

I didn't know love required a name. You taught me.

At times she marvels at her pedigree . . .

The war ended on the eleventh hour of the eleventh day of the eleventh month.

On the seventh day of that month, a little girl was born.

On the eighteenth day of the eighth month twenty-two years later, a little girl was born.

On the fifth day of the second month thirty-one years later, a little girl was born.

. . . and falls hard . . .

There are no books, no conversations, no games, no dinner plans.

There are two channels, but one of them has really bad reception. Something to do with the way a satellite is oriented on top of the sky.

It is nice to think about the satellite, but it is nicer to watch the first channel, which has better reception.

The remote isn't as remote as it sounds, and the buttons are big and hard to push, which is why you don't bother with the buttons anymore.

When I talk to you, we have a three-way conversation with the TV.

. . . and harder still.

The cleaning lady, who comes twice a week, is an opera singer.

She is not really a cleaning lady, but more of an opera singer doing some housekeeping. She doesn't dust very well, and a lot of things are sticky in the kitchen. The dinner table has a crack. The lamp on the commode misses a bulb. There is a little stagnant pool in the shower.

The opera singer knows not to unsettle things. When she

comes in, she holds your fingers between hers as in a sand-wich. She calls you Madame Gerard. Sometimes she will lay a hand on your shoulder and tell you stories of her heart.

She doesn't come on Wednesdays.

Come Wednesday and she visits . . .

Beside the hat shop, where the street is so narrow and lush with your late friend Sylvie's heady fragrance, shining in all their glory in the Pauvert deli display, two lobster tails, exposing their cooked insides and how they were cushioned in cascades of mayonnaise ribbons topped with carrot dice and two green peas, hijacked me and my wallet into the line to Mrs. Pauvert's cash register.

Wednesday morning turned out to be heavy with two cellophaned scavengers and the thought of making you satiated.

"Catch your breath" was what pedestrians told me with their eyes as though breath was this thing that could be caught.

Now I walk in the wake of the invisible vapor that comes once into my nose and twice out of my mouth.

Up the hill the idea of the glass door to your building is more real than the real thing, and I am waiting long before I wait by the buzzer.

Opening your door takes a million years.

. . . and remembers—such is life a multiplication of memories . . .

Many Wednesdays ago I took you to the tiny museum with three stories and one elevator.

It was hard and funny to fit you and the wheelchair into the elevator. Up we went in a whoosh.

On the top floor was a flock of Rodin hand studies.

You and I strolled through the forest of hands and walked out untouched, both of us unaware that the world was anything besides a forest of hands.

. . . divided by impossible wishes . . .

Two cities you have never been to: New York and San Francisco.

You tell me your wish and immediately you forget because you're too busy emptying the carcass of a cooked lobster.

Awful cracking of your jaws as I sit wondering how much longer you will hold your thought, whether it is indeed a thought, or just hyphenation, and whether I should reignite you with a word or a question or the aggravation of me cutting my salad leaves.

Then I say those are two cities that have straight lines for streets, and inside I am very scared that you will lose your denture.

. . . and derisory wills . . .

"Take care of your mother, will you?"

And I don't say: "Because you didn't?"

"Your father can be careless in some respects."

And I don't say: "And you were too."

"She did not forgive Gerard, even on his deathbed."

And I don't say: "And she won't forgive you."

"Your mother's father never brought me a present when on leave."

And I don't say: "As a result he exploded on a roadside bomb and you wedded Gerard."

Instead I say: "What a jerk my grandfather!"

And we laugh.

. . . offset by small bubbles . . .

Some people like air bubbles in their finished glass pieces.

But most people think of bubbles as a nuisance.

Sometimes an unfired sheet of glass will have small bubbles captured inside. These bubbles are called seeds.

Large bubbles occasionally break through to form a hole.

A way to attack this problem is to slow down the fusing schedule.

In the commode, there is a set of Czech glasses with air bubbles in different colors.

Some Kafkaesque glass blower in his primitive workshop turned imperfection into art.

. . . and the possibility . . .

Your recliner isn't reclined, and you sit on it like a Japanese wave about to crash.

Despite that posture you're taking a nap.

Think of a Japanese wave held in momentum and forbidden to crash.

I sit cross-legged at the trough and read a Catholic newspaper, which has an article on spelling.

It says nowadays students are no longer penalized for wrong spelling.

I look up at you and decide it would be best to kill you today.

. . . of outward euthanasia.

Bock, bock, bock, begowwwk.

During wartime a brave little chicken was making noises at the bottom of a potato sack.

Miles away stood a house and a kitchen where a vigorous mistress held a knife that could use some sharpening.

"Remember the old rooster," clucked the brave little chicken in his despair as he banged on the back of a girl on a bicycle.

The old rooster had escaped the strangler's hands for one entire night.

The old rooster was a believer, and while the world suffered in judgment, he had stood forth on the roof among the anointed of the chicken God.

The rooster was no chicken, and yet the little chicken took heart in that recollection.

The rooster had looked up at the stars, which were put out one by one as the night faded into dawn.

Now the valiant chicken had only darkness, yet his entire route was illumined.

Is there dignity in dying? she asks . . .

I am eight years old.

You make me sleep on a cot next to you and Gerard. One of you is snoring.

The blinds let a bit of light in at the bottom, yet there is no air because you keep the windows shut at night.

Volutes of heat come from the floor, encasing us like Christmas presents.

The eight-year-old me wishes to be in Morocco watching the dancing cigarette tip of my mother.

The eight-year-old me wishes to pee, but the toilet lock is hard.

Now the two of you are snoring.

"Grandma?"

"Yes."

"Are you sleeping?"

"No."

"And you, Gerard?"

"No."

"Can we play Rami?"

. . . or dignity in the acknowledgment of incompetence?

You were eight years old.

I made you sleep on a medical bed with rails so you wouldn't escape.

Before that, I had washed you with a mitt. I had lifted and adjusted the giant diaper on your hips.

Your nightie was a bit wet, but the other one wasn't dry yet, and the third one was way too warm for August.

We therefore agreed to lay a towel on the bed that would absorb any excess.

Before that, I had washed your teeth and rubbed them with a piece of charcoal for about thirty seconds. I was careful not to brush your gums.

We agreed that white is better than yellow.

Before that, we had made plans for next Wednesday.

We agreed that a tour on the lake would be wonderful but that if the weather was rotten, it would be best to go to the movies.

After that, I laid your pillbox and a glass of water on your night table and kissed you on both cheeks.

We agreed that drugs were nice, although wine had a better taste.

You didn't say: "Would you please kill me tonight?"

I didn't say: "I'd be happy to, but how?"

You didn't say: "Never mind."

After that, I waited until you started snoring before I shut your door behind me.

The Bond

He had this exquisite and disturbing gesture, my brother-in-law Max. Here it is: in a delicately carved and painted chest, hand delivered by private courier: a collection of pictures, drawings, and representations of my sister Mia throughout the twenty-five years of their married life. Max wanted me to have this. In the cover note, he explained that nothing was missing from that collection, not one sketch or one painting or one figurine of her that he'd done or attempted over the course of their coexistence. There was no insignificant corner of paper tablecloth on which he drew her on the spot that Max didn't religiously keep and unearth from the grave of memories. All of Mia's evolution over those years was captured with exceptional clarity, structured in binders and small cardboard cases tied with knotted, colored strings, like an elaborate interlocked molecular construction.

What I thought was lost and erased with Mia's death was here, methodically and artistically arranged; her renditions protected with rice paper and silicon packets. All of this obsessive minutia had an intoxicating yet distancing effect on me—like a train of feelings with vastly different wagons, through which I could stroll as a visitor to my own interior world. My old self opened every sleeve, unwrapped every package with an all-consuming adolescent fever. The great distance of age and the scorching nearness of juvenile fervor were back-to-back, holding each other's weight.

As I laid those Mias on my dinner table, like a mosaic of mirrors, I had to smile. Was this Mia? Did she age so well—gaining with maturity a polished gloss that made her almost liquid? I was in the same denial I had experienced once: This couldn't be my sister, a woman made with the same blood that I felt burning inside me; conceivably she was a sibling, but that was just how others would perceive her, not who I knew she was, in the private cockpit of my skin. And so Max, the painter and sculptor who had spent so much of his life trying to pierce the secret of Mia by stealing and appropriating her image, had glanced over her essence, the compressed spring from which every movement started. Very little of Mia had escaped Max, and surely that was what had kept his love of her so fresh, so unconditional. Max knew.

The Mias from the chest understood that, and were at peace with Max's knowledge. I could see that. Yet I felt the necessity to add my piece to this collection, the one that would make all of them alive again. I sat before the table and closed my eyes. I needed to revisit the few hours that counted, the ones that had crystallized the brutal and crisp impulse that would inhabit me and make her. I had them coming down on me like a heavy rain, inescapable, like droplets exploding upward as they hit the ground. The light and the music were in the droplets. All I had to do was let loose, recount our story to myself, out of love for her, the purest feeling from my youth.

∿

I saw Mia for the first time in a small provincial clinic. To me the clinic wasn't small and provincial; to me the clinic was big, colossal as a pantheon. Four of me stacked on top of each other would fit through the entrance. My father took me there, holding my toddler hand. It was a rare instance: my father holding my hand. The moment was solemn, filled with nurses murmuring in the hallways like people whispering in churches. There was an elevator, and my father lifted me up to press the button. This was my first elevator. Now that I think of it, I think of all maternities as elevated, hovering above ground.

The elevator transported us to a new hallway with a door at the end. I wondered what could be behind the door that my father opened with such care. From across the room, I saw Mia in the arms of my mother and asked my father who she was. My father responded with something that I didn't hear. My father repeated the same thing and I still couldn't hear. My mother smiled and called me to her. I approached the bed and was encouraged to sit on it. I touched Mia's hand. I was told her name.

"Mia?" I asked.

"Yes. Kiss her," my mother said.

And I obeyed my mother.

There are certain quakes, ways to be moved that recounted would verge on the sentimental; certain words and gestures that sound true only once, as they spark out of the unexpected morass of feelings. For me, kissing Mia at the clinic was the first shaking; a shaking that left me in a state of questioning, a state that I haven't left yet.

❧

After that there was a long stretch of years where nothing happened. I saw my sister every day, and the routine had buried the kiss at the clinic, folded it in some remote emotional drawer. Until that summer.

Our closeness was reignited in the warm water of a bath. It was a peaceful evening, stretching at the end of a day with no school. The bathroom windows were wide open, and through their dark frames, the dusky sky floated in as the vapor from the bath escaped. My mother had appointed me to watch Mia. It wasn't customary for me to watch Mia taking a bath, although it wasn't the first time.

It is strange how you forget to look at what you constantly have before your eyes, how it becomes part of a private scenery, invisible, until you are being asked to watch. That evening, perhaps out of a sense of duty, I started watching Mia in the bathtub.

She was still little, maybe five. Her hands were playing

with the edge of the tub. The water had softened her skin to the point that it was wrinkled and much lighter in color—almost lilac. After a few minutes of watching her hands, I remember feeling swallowed into my own focus, absorbed into magnetic observation. I moved my face closer, so as to look at Mia's fingers from under a mental microscope. It wasn't exceptional: me getting into this dreamlike zone. I was the sort of child to experience rapture: my own mind flying above myself. But never had I seen Mia's skin so close, like an elemental phenomenon. Without knowing I was moving, under an urge deeper than simple curiosity, somewhat like a sleepwalker, I was pushed magically toward a narrow circle inches from her hands. I was carried away by the movement of her fingers, the unended circle of her fingerprints, the delicate nuances beneath her nails.

Our story could have ended there. My mother could have called us. Mia could have laughed out loud or thrown water at my face. That ecstatic moment would have been submerged like an Atlantis under the waves of family reality, lost forever. Instead Mia's right hand got away from the edge of the tub, and she placed a finger on one of my eyebrows. In a slow motion, she traced the line as if she was drawing me. It was a childish gesture, but it carried a depth that made my world suddenly larger, more tender.

I am not sure I knew in that moment that new possibilities were emerging out of the bathwater, that emotional islands materialized under Mia's forefinger, drifting to form a continent. It is easy for me to recognize it now. It is easy to become your own historian with the help of a lifelong telescope. Part of the magic, however, is to be ignorant at first of the pivotal seconds that make you. As I now realize, the first lines of my drama had just been traced by Mia.

Did we stay in the bathroom for much longer? Did Mia feel as I did a sudden expansion of our cosmos? Can one explain such changes?

That evening, I remember staying in my room, pretending to be sick. I didn't have dinner. My first move was to unearth from my desk the few drawings and birthday cards that Mia had given me over the years. From one moment to the next, I uncovered in them a new universe; Mia's tenderness was rushing toward me as if it had been looking for me forever; her pictures and words were running, taking me along like a wave, deep in the stream of my veins. I was feeling a dizziness similar to the one that can be felt in a dream when one dreams of flying. My legs were shaking, but other than their motion, I felt paralyzed; nothing like this had ever happened to me, and it was all under the effect of a simple sisterly gesture. But the gesture stayed with me, and the thought of it was intoxicating, so much so that I was trying to repeat it, my own finger tracing my brow in the same slow motion. In the span of a few hours, the wall that separated me from Mia had been taken down, and I discovered in myself a new intensity.

I became worried for Mia and her own feelings. And as I worried, I waited. I was waiting for her to wake up and come down for breakfast. I was waiting for her to come back from school. I was waiting for her to look at me, to talk to me, to lift a finger; to see if the gesture from the bath would be repeated, and with it the warm vibe that had seized me and lifted me up to a place of passion and grace. My eyes would land on her, always more anxious, probing her face, sometimes estranged and disappointing; while her features were undeniably the same, she would be devoid of the tender strength I had seen. Her face would be weary and common, as if she was putting on the mask of an unknown and prematurely old child. I didn't understand how that could be: her duality. Although duality was at the core of her, I could see it as I started to truly look. Mia's eyes were dark yet luminous; her short light hair was flowing toward her forehead in a hasty attempt to hide its audacity. Her pointed chin was split; she would start a smile and soon cancel it. Every piece of her was loaded with ambiguity, and I've never known anyone more mobile, more changing. Now I know that certain bubbling of the spirit can transform a face, yielding a splendor or ugliness that the years cannot.

But it was too soon, I wasn't ready to accept Mia's coming and going, my own internal clouds only dissipating when she would deign to shine on me like a lazy sun. I chose to flee.

∾

Seven years later we were taking a vacation on a small and sunny island in the south. My parents had allowed me to take a friend along so that I would not feel too isolated. I had a friend named Matthias. Matthias and I were roommates in the boarding school that I had attended since the summer of the bathroom incident. I wanted him with me during that vacation, to shield me from myself. Every summer until that one had been a torture, enduring in the face of Mia the lightning that she'd throw abundantly without knowing. Seeing her after a long stretch of absence meant that I was electrically charged, exposed. Every time I had hoped that I would stop feeling what I felt. Every time her apparition would annihilate that hope. I was terrorized that all my bottled-up passion would pop a cork and wound her, because I couldn't care less about my own wounds, and also quite frankly because I kept licking my blood like a bee feeding on nectar.

That summer started splendidly, with such treacherous beauty! The insular air was blinding and heavy with invisible particles; Matthias and I would squint our eyes, perched on boulders, ready to dive in a perfect crescent; we'd jump and elevate our bodies before hitting the water headfirst. Infinite water stretched before us and under us, sometimes inside us, as we'd drink the cup in a dizzying race across the bay. The island soil was rammed hard and fine, like rice powder; and we grappled in reckless marathons, risking our lives along the cliff with juvenile madness. On the vertical rock faces and horizontal overhangs, we proclaimed ourselves the gods of free-climbing, relying on our fingers and toes to overcome perpendicular nightmares.

Our interminable tests of strength finished us off breathless and leaning on the oak tree trunks overlooking a purple sunset. Matthias rarely broke the silence, and his quietness was reassuring and comfortable.

For the first time in ages, I was untroubled, happy. And I wasn't interested in knowing why. I had forgotten everything, fully immersed in my body and its contact with the elements. My tensed muscles kept asking me what I could do next that would be bolder and riskier.

In hindsight, I can see that this was one more escape attempt from Mia's chiaroscuro gaze over the dinner table. But in the deepness of those summer hours, I felt freer from her; I thought I was getting detached, earning back my body inch by inch along with the hushed lightness of friendship.

As for Matthias, he seemed immune to girls, or if he wasn't, he was very discreet about it. It isn't hard to understand why I liked that about him. But it is hard to imagine sexual indifference in a young and strong body; Matthias seemed to be a specimen. He was from a Nordic family, with a bulging and wide forehead, straight eyebrows sloping up toward the center, and pale gray eyes lined with generous upper and lower eyelids, which seemed to make him constantly smile. Indeed he smiled a lot, although rarely showing his teeth; and that joyous disposition came under a long and thin nose, slightly scarred in the middle like one of a boxer. Matthias was extremely good-looking in an understated way.

Two weeks had gone by with exhilarating physicality and unparalleled freedom. Vacations were coming to an end, and days seemed imperceptibly shorter. I anticipated the next term with dread, since I loved that island intermission so much, and the subterranean atmosphere of the school and dorm threatened me with a deportation from my newly revealed body. I was sharing with Matthias secret conspiracies that would make us prolong our stay, which he received with a benevolent smile. But the moment of our departure had been assigned by fate, and that hour was hanging over me like a sharp pendulum, bearing in its blade the inevitable stroke of midnight.

I decided that our last night on the island would be in the wild. We would sleep in the small eastern cove only accessible at low tide. There only, cradled with the lapping of the waves, we would make an honorable exit. I am not ashamed of my youthful pomposity, because it was truly innocent. My theatrical sense wanted to pay tribute to the elements that had given me such vigor.

We took heavy covers and bottled water, and waved goodbye to my parents. Mia wasn't in sight, which I almost didn't notice.

To this day and from that night, I bear in me a bitter-sweet taste for sleeping in the open. Every evening when the time comes, I am surprised by my willingness to lie in bed covered with a ceiling; a ceiling on which a face can so easily form as condensation and come down—down—and still down on me like in the classic tale of torture.

That night, as Matthias and I sat and then lay on the sand, the vaulted darkness folded at the edges where it met the ocean. There was no limit to our breaths, no limit to the words we exchanged about ourselves, about our take on the universe. Everything including us could go the distance, and I wanted to never find sleep amidst the flooding quietness of that summer night. How I wanted to hold the fort of those hours with my friend! Instead a much-undesired sleep found me.

And hours later it was the silence that woke me. Wasn't there someone else next to us? I opened my eyes slowly and just halfway. I observed with such rigid anxiety that my eyes started to water. Something icy and implacable was running up my naked legs. An intruder, an assassin could come near us soundlessly like that. Yes, there was some-one next to Matthias who seemed to be kneeling, like in prayer, but without the hands extended. The arms were on the sides and then floating to hover over Matthias's face and his torso, hesitant and ill assured. I knew the contours of that shadow. Was it Mia? No, it wasn't her demeanor, the indecision, the cowardly slowness of the moves. Then through the shutters of my eyes, still pretending to be asleep, I saw Matthias sit up like a ghost and grab the head gently by the hair to bring it to his face.

I was shaking, mortified. I could only lift my upper body onto my elbows and mutter inanely: "What are you doing?"

They got out of their embrace and looked at me without talking; something was also depriving them of speech. Finally Mia put a hand in her hair to brush it away from her face, and the moonlight caught her temples and the bridge of her nose. At last, she stuttered: "I wanted . . . I wanted . . ."

Her voice was faltering. She was there, kneeling, eyes lowered, like a thief caught red-handed. That anxiety, our standoff, me frozen under my blankets, her shriveled into herself and stunned by shame, was unbearable. Matthias tried to put an end to it: "Listen, it's fine, we just kissed, we both wanted to kiss."

Suddenly the weak silhouette got up from its kneeling position. She came closer to me, with a mean smile, a smile that was visible in the eyes only, shining like those of a crouched cat, and for a moment she looked like an African demon mask, suspended above me in the night sky; and then her smoky voice floated to me like a curse escaping from her pinched lips: "Yes, I wanted to kiss . . . you understand? I wanted to kiss . . . Matthias is a good kisser . . . you see . . . I liked kissing him . . . maybe I'll do it again."

She was staring at me with such cruelty, like a slap across my face, and her fingers were curled in a fist, ready to punch. I wanted to be swallowed in the sand under me. Was she crazy? But this only lasted one second. Then Mia pivoted onto herself and walked away from us, her blonde hair slowly shrinking into the night until it became a dot at the end of my vision.

∽

In light of such history, wasn't it absurd that I chose to attend university in the small provincial town of my parents? I could have moved to the capital, where I was accepted; I could even have moved abroad for a year or two; instead I decided to stay there, in agreement with both my father and mother on this. Back then I would never acknowledge to myself what it really was: a camouflaged attempt to be closer to Mia once again—just a few miles away—after years of avoidance. Over the years, our occasional encounters during special family events had been like stirring an iceberg, where one can watch slabs of ice crash down into a milky gray lake and find more ice beyond the fallen ice. But now I felt older, quieter, more mature; I could "take it." Also I had a few days to get acclimated; Mia had been sent away for the summer and wouldn't be back in town until after my first week.

Oh, my choice seemed hardly questionable, even to myself. The local university had a grand reputation, in great contrast with the raggedness of its buildings. And after years in the obscure and remote boarding school, with nothing to offer but a flawless academic record, this seemed like a step up into a wild, wide-open world. Upon my first visit to the campus, I sensed that circles of friends and acquaintances were formed fast and without effort; that they were mobile and could be undone or reshaped as fast as they assembled. This was dizzying in a way that I liked. In a

matter of hours, I had taken a tour, which included enroll-
ment in all the courses I was interested in and checking the
buildings where I would take them. The only place I hadn't
checked was the library. I was told it was closed for a conference that day until four. I was there at four sharp after
a quick stroll through the city of my childhood, which felt
small and foreign yet distantly familiar, as if I was drunk
while taking a tour of my own house, little details popping
up absurdly before my befuddled eyes.

I came through the library door, and inside it was silent.
The reading room was empty and well lit, with red chairs
and blacktop tables. I picked up a book at random and
sat, pretending to study. And soon someone came in, and
someone else, and again and again until the room was half
full. Every now and then, I would lift my eyes from the
book and look around, checking if anyone looked interesting. I was in a social mood, ready to break into a conversation like one shakes the numbness of their legs.

Legs were what I saw first as she sat across the table,
swinging them on to the side. She had the thin and nervous muscles of an adolescent, maybe a bit too thin. As I
looked up from my book, Mia was staring at me mockingly.
Then the corner of her lips subsided and her eyes opened
up, and she put on a disarming look of sincerity, one that
would take no tall story. "Well, I've been looking for you!
But where else could you have been? It has been awhile,
hasn't it? Shall we have a coffee?"

Humbled and without will, I allowed myself to be carried along by her outside the library into a popular cafeteria. There, in the deafening cacophony of students' declarations and cheap music, I asked Mia a dozen silly questions to which she responded wholeheartedly and with unexpected openness. I was at once troubled and content; her voice did that to me. She spoke with a certain haste and ease about indifferent things, and I was grateful that she had not paid attention to my temporary discomfort, that she had forgotten it.

It baffles me that I can't remember the name of that cafeteria where we ended up spending so much time that fall, and honestly I don't—I've buried it at the bottom of an internal ocean where the soil is smooth and abyssal. Was it named after its owner? Or a place? Or a time? I will call it the C.

From our encounters at the C., which soon became a weekly ritual, a new way to observe Mia started for me; until then, my veneration for her had been mostly imaginative; by that I mean that all that moved me about her was crafted and sublime, exempt from materiality. I hadn't dared to envisage what her days were like; and this had been made easy by years of separation. Mia had been the receptacle of poetry, the messianic queen sent to save me. The world and its objects were nostalgic rubbles ennobled by the possibility of her traveling through them: a fig tree odor, a dark shade of yellow, an ant walking between the floorboards, salted almonds, a big sky. With the exaggeration characteristic of the overfocused, I had meticulously wiped off any concrete detail of her existence. I had lost any notion of how she spent time, where she got her hair cut, what she liked to eat. And so, in the same way that a child born deaf can only hear what sounds like a muted piano, and all the noises he can imagine are trills and scales from the same instrument, I never envisioned her being other than transcendent and cruel and innocent. Never before had I thought of Mia in terms of simple material constraints, physical obligations, weekly schedule. Now in the course of our discussions at the C., she was placing all of that in front of me as if we had been lifelong friends: her small high school stories, her quick-witted jokes, her impulsive maternal temper. One foggy but still warm afternoon in the second week of the term, she confided how she had to sleep on her back since she had bruised her rib cage while rummaging in a trash can looking for a hairpin.

From then on and much against my will, I was compelled to take in all the particulars of her life. Why was she so accessible when she had been so fearfully deep, incomprehensible? The more Mia shared with me, the more unsettled I was. There was no apparent tension, no ostentatious expression of distress; on the contrary, there was a warm disposition, an opaque complicity growing between us, and the nature of that made the atmosphere calm yet weighted and stormy, less bearable than a cloud bursting. From the outside, nothing betrayed us—we looked content, and perhaps I thought we were, but that was only the bloated look of the starving.

Amidst that tension, I was struck by Mia's solitude. Often on the weekends, she would stay entire days without getting out of the house, or only to bike the distance for coffee at the C.

Midway through the first quarter, I became invested in trying to break that seclusion. And one day over coffee, I invited her to an upcoming dance.

∾

It was a mild fall day; the light and warmth of it had settled in the air with a thin veil of lightheartedness. A young moon was there, with a barely visible halo crescent, as if self-conscious of its own glow. Obscurity was moving in on us as we walked through town to the campus where the party would take place. Mia didn't speak. She was wearing a polka dot black-and-white dress with a black cardigan and flats. The fading light seemed to be brushing her face from underneath her, her skin and hair intensified as if captured through a camera obscura. I felt complete. I felt in the walking by her side that life was giving me the ultimate accomplishment. Why? Because in walking next to her through the descending evening, we belonged to each other in our parallel paths, and what else could I do to top that? From the second we stopped walking till the day I died, I'd live knowing that this moment would belong to a sepia-colored place in my soul. I knew it with the same vividness as the mystery of faith revealed, and the realization brought me a pleasure only found in the darkness of repression, a pain as sacred as the restraint preventing it from being manifested.

Somewhere in my looks, troubled and moved, Mia read an invitation.

"Come, let's sit on this bench . . . we don't have to go right now . . . please sit near me . . . no, not like that . . . please do not look at me, or I won't be able to talk."

Night had fallen by then, and the bench was far from any streetlight. I sensed Mia very close to me, through her breathing, a bit heavy, getting lost in the dark. Then her voice rose and murmured so low I could barely hear: "I . . . love you . . . not in the way I'm supposed to."

Did I flinch? Did those words spark an instinctive physical retreat from the shock? I must have made some gesture of withdrawal or surprise, because I felt her collapsing and moving away, like someone shunned and punished. "Do you despise me now?" she asked almost inaudibly. "Are you horrified now?"

Why couldn't I find a word? Why did I stay mute, as if indifferent, embarrassed, numbed, instead of showing her that I cared beyond anything she could imagine? Instead, all the moments with Mia flushed by in a torrential outpour and had this chilling effect, as if the code behind them was suddenly decrypted; I understood Mia with terrible clarity: our first kiss at the clinic, her tender gliding over my brow from the warmth of the bathtub, her hatred as she kissed another to provoke me, her tenacious and glacial flight from my ever-growing tenderness during my rare visits, her openness at the C., and the hope that friendship would kill love. Her love, I had always sensed it on me, shy or passionate, tender or cruel; I had rolled in its dew. However, when she pronounced the word, from lips that looked exceedingly similar to mine, with a sensual inflection, I felt a tremor at once soft and petrifying, some throbbing gush behind my temples. And despite my passion for her, me, the young, estranged, distraught, and unspoken lover, wracked and shivering, I couldn't find one word to respond to her declaration.

She was sitting, hunched, shattered by my silence: "Is it so terrifying? So terrifying?" she uttered. "You won't forgive me . . . ? Well, it's better that you know now; now it's not so oppressive. Anything is better than this repression and counterfeiting. It's better to stop it right there . . ."

How much sadness was in her words, how much resignation! The vibration of her voice was traveling beyond my skin, gliding in my blood, piercing me with shame for staying so cold, so confined in front of a woman who had given me more than anyone and who was humiliating herself before me. I wanted to speak, I wanted to respond, I wanted to shout, but I was trapped in the glass bubble of appearances, and my mouth wouldn't obey me. I felt pitifully small and embarrassed, so much so that Mia tried to give me courage: "Don't just stay like that, atrociously still. Please get a grip on yourself. Are you so ashamed of me? Now I said it. Let's at least part ways with respect, like friends, like family . . ."

I couldn't find any strength, let alone any collectedness; Mia had triggered what looked like infinite passivity and what concealed unlimited panic. I was confronted, exposed; and so was the unbearable weight of my feelings. I had revered them while they remained wisely underneath; I had cocooned and nourished them like soft animals. And now Mia was tearing the skin on my chest open and baring the eye of the unspoken. In that moment I hated being scared, I hated my cowardice, I hated my own hatred. But Mia, who was faster, had already forgiven me. She touched my arm gently and stood up. I sensed her in the darkness going to the other side of the bench and sitting on the ground, her back to my back. "Is it better like that?" she asked.

Now that I think of it, I picture us on either side of that bench as the two faces of the same being, nondifferent like a fire and its heat, like one having taken two forms to allow the exchange of feelings.

And there Mia's voice arose again, and she told me everything.

Mia divulged herself to me in complete nakedness; she avidly exposed the premises for her torment, the self-doubts and the self-loathing, the turpitudes of her heart, the meanderings of her desires, the ever-growing clarity of her condition. There was a wild sensuality in her confession—a bold womanliness. Only one who has been deeply ashamed can delve with near drunkenness into cruel self-incrimination. Bit by bit, Mia tore out the layers like heavy clothes in the heat. And with a haggard look and teary eyes, I saw for the first time the immeasurable richness of her being—and the far greater complexity of what bound us.

Oh, her voice in the night, her voice in the darkness! I felt it drilling into the coatings of my fear; like a missile bird across the layers of air and water. Soon it would resonate as my own, as if I was telling the words. I could tell her story through her lips, my own lips moving at the same time, knowing the words before she pronounced them. And at some point, I must have spoken along with her, like overtone singing on the other side of the bench, like another self.

Then our voices ceased to be heard and only darkness remained. I knew she was there, behind the wooden slats of the bench. I could just extend my hand and touch her. But again she was the first to move and stood up, exhausted, staggering slowly toward me. I stood up too, lifted up by some dreamlike force. And the obscure instinct that was usually clouded by the weight of self-consciousness had gained brilliance and sharpness, like a tiny blue flame on a candlewick. She pulled me into her, and I pulled her into me; our lips joined in a nervous tremor.

It was a kiss like no other, a desperate and voracious kiss, like an embrace in the face of death. We were letting go of who we had been, and the fear of what would become of us was the living breath of our hunger.

When we finally released each other, like in a seizure,

with throbbing pain, we stepped back and stood up straight, facing each other as if looking into a fateful mirror. Gradually I felt her body become heavier, and her head started shaking a bit. I moved forward and took her head in my hands and kissed her again. Kissed her. Again.

I abducted my sister to my dorm room.

The moments that followed belong to memory even before they became memory. They were the carnal unwinding of our history. Perhaps we remembered them long before they existed. Perhaps our remembrance made them exist. Ashes to ashes, flesh to flesh. Through the stubborn frame of that reminiscence, I conceive of our lovemaking as a medieval fresco: with an outburst of violence, both savage and codified. I see us as two groups rather than two beings; two similar formations moving forward, then dismantling under the shock before regrouping for a new assault. That night, we consumed our love. Completely alone and together; two wings—torn from our togetherness, bloodied and miraculous—knowing we'd never fly again—knowing we'd always be flying. Mia's salt on her skin, the taste of amber on my lips, Mia's eyes looking nowhere, my omniscient blindness. How long did it last? At what point did we lose the grace? At what exact moment did we disentangle ourselves from each other?

Still today, it is the after that I fear the most. The time of loss: when our eyes met and paused; when our eyes, now empty of the blindness, saw again. How could we tolerate it? The shame. As soon as the heat of our bodies ceased to trouble our senses, I let go of her. It was like the violent jolt of a fractured body. With ache, I sat up and turned my back to her. It lasted a few minutes, my inert body having nothing in front but void, my bed abruptly altered into the edge of a bottomless pit. Slowly my head became too heavy, rolled forward, along with my shoulders, conceding to fatigue and exhaustion; and then, like a weight too heavy oscillating for too long between two positions that topples all of a sudden into the slope, I let go of my upper body forward and folded in two, my head between my knees, my hands sweeping the wooden slats on the floor.

I felt Mia ruffling in the sheets, moving toward me. And I bounced back up, as if in a last convulsion. I turned toward her with my hands clasped on my face like a mask, and I heard my own voice: throaty and vaguely menacing: "Go away . . . go away . . . do not come near . . . for the love of us both . . . go now . . . go!"

She understood. She always understood. She left like a runaway; leaving tenuous hints of herself on a once beloved land.

∾

We never saw each other again. Our parents suffered terribly from it. They never understood what could have driven us to that iron will of separateness. We offered no explanation. Their obstinacy could not drill any closer to the fiery core that they must have sensed. Maybe they drilled away from their intuition. How would one expect them to do otherwise? We had to make complex plans to attend their funerals separately. What happened between Mia and me remained forever trapped like an air bubble under an oceanic boulder. Only my brother-in-law Max must have glimpsed what had been.

Max helped remarkably; he wrote to me on and off; he called throughout the years to keep me posted on the important things: the wedding, the children, Mia's artistic accomplishments. He never asked any questions.

I even met him a few times, and I learned to like him, to love him—perhaps a bit like my sister did. And today again, sitting before his many representations of her, at my dinner table, with more clarity than the young shaking brother I was then, I know I owe Mia everything I was and have become; since that night of fifty years ago where she opened us up like one inserts a knife into a resilient oyster shell, any true expression of love has carried the echo of that moment. Since that night, I owe my sister the trust I have in my ever-enduring capacity to love.

And it is me: that feeling and that trust. A "me" that I had almost forgotten, buried as it was in intricate shells of adulthood and ripeness. Yet it was always so present and so pressing. It is the only possible me, pushing against a frame that has taken years to build, celebrating the frame as one more piece of its own edifice. All my life, I have loved and created and given in memoriam of that feeling. Not out of grief though. I was and still am burning its very alive truth serum. I was never alone. Mia's breath was behind my own, inside my own; and in recalling our times, I want to give her my blood, to my love, my own flesh, so that it can speak and sing again and so that she, now gone since yesterday, can lie again next to me as I age.

The Point of No Return

Later, in two weeks, I would come back home—almost thirty-eight and I would come back home, in two weeks, after this vacation, before the month's end.

I am thinking it's not funny, and inevitably it makes me laugh. I have been laughing a lot, randomly, often, for almost thirty-eight years. Although I don't know if I laughed much as an infant, before I remember me being me. But I guess I did. I can forge a memory of my first serious fit of laughter when I was ten months old, a laughter that surprised my father and my mother, a laughter that was way too deep for a baby, way too inexplicable, something freed in this tiny body: *poof*—a surprise—the world held in that laughter, the promise of the world and just the end of it. I hesitate to name this laughter a conclusion, but in my case it's been a conclusion—albeit fragile—not a very solid conclusion. Somewhere on my horizon there is a freewheeling fit of laughter disconnected from its source.

In the early weeks of the trip, before I got sick, I see him: the guide we'd hired for the tour of the island. I think he liked me very much. Nothing predestined him to like me. He was very small, perhaps not even five feet, very mis-

chievous; while I am very tall, five feet eleven; too tall for
my size and not completely comfortable with it. I tend to
slouch a little to compensate; obviously I never wear heels.
I think in the beginning he liked me because I seemed to
be listening. I asked questions, a lot of them, and waited for
his answers, and listened to them, patiently, with a small
elusive smile. The smile wasn't coquetry, it was just a smile;
I am not sure how else to look, a smile here or there seems
the polite thing to do as I listen. He may have misinter-
preted the smile, but upon reflection I think not. I think it
was something else, or the sum of a lot of small things. My
sister, who has been with me on this trip, believes in dramatic pivotal moments; she is a first-kiss, last-breath type.
I veer toward the theory of hydrodynamics: a small angle
of helm to create a shift, the sum of small angles to make a
turn. It's essentially the same thing, pivotal moments and
the sum of small angles, all a matter of perspective, of one's
distance toward change.

For the record: I never thought of myself as particularly
pretty. I think of myself as *me*, without a lot of qualifiers.
Only the things I'm not completely comfortable with are
noticeable to me, such as my size. I don't dislike myself
in a mirror, but I detest myself in a picture. I don't mind
my own voice, but I hate being recorded and played back.
I accept my own smell, as long as I can forget it. I never
wear perfumes that are too strong. I'd have to really sniff
my own neck to know which one I am wearing, or if I'm
wearing one at all. I don't mind the shape of my ears, as

long as they're hidden under my hair. I hide the white in my hair because I am not yet used to the old me. I lost my big toenail a long time ago; I hide it under an acrylic substitute. I have an obsession with my absent toenail which is always noticeable.

The name of the guide was Ketut (*Qi-toot*), which means "fourth child." It turns out this small island has come up with an incredibly complex calendar and an equally simplistic system to name people. The calendar consists of ten concurrent weeks of one to ten days each; each day out of the two hundred and ten possible permutations is a unique blend of days picked from each different week. While the days of most weeks are arranged in simple recurring cycles, the order in three of the weeks are subject to obscure calculations. By contrast, the fourth child is always *Ketut*. So days are more unique than people, which, upon thinking it through, makes sense.

Ketut liked to preserve his effects. By that I mean both stylistic effects and effects of surprise—effects in general. For example, I would ask a question and he would answer that he would not answer but rather save his answer for later during the trip. He'd say his answer would only make sense in its context. He would not talk about temples before we actually set foot in one. He would not talk about cremation ceremonies before we attended one. I tempted a joke and said that, strictly speaking, he should not speak about cremation until we could fully experience it. This earned me a short silence and possibly one point on the Ke-tut Scale. *It's very complicated*, Ketut said. *Very complicated*, he repeated. I could not be sure what he was referring to. What was so complicated?

By the end of week one, I'd learn all there was to learn about growing rice and the various stages of the crop. We had hiked through a great number of rice terraces. We had biked through them. We had had lunch overlooking them. We had slept in bungalows adjacent to them. Perhaps the proximity of rice in its various stages of growth, and the focus required to not fall into the glossy mud beneath the lush green of the fields, lulled me into a certain breed of anxiety, something unnamed and inherently nostalgic. I had the distinct and very conscious feeling of this being the last time. *This is the last time*, I'd keep thinking in loops, *the last time*. If Ketut had been the one thinking or saying it, he would have added his favorite question—*do you understand what I mean?* A phrase he always added after his most incomprehensible diatribes.

Of course I know that every time is the last time. But there has been something circular in this trip, and in that circularity there's also an end, a tip, a bottommost point. That's what has been troubling me in the rice fields.

Once during one of the hikes we crossed a group of peas-ants, resting in the shade on the side of a small hut, shelter-ing a cow. The cow was splendid. Her brown skin looked impossibly tender, like a rug slowly baked under the sun. Of course I wanted to rest my feet on her. She seemed to be looking at nothing specific, and I took a mental picture of her nebulous eyes. I never take real pictures. I hate the time and distance stolen by the camera from the experience. But I've kept that mental picture. I would hold onto that one in particular. I think I've lost a lot of memories lately. But that one is here with me, dark and warm and liquid. It makes me smaller than I really am, more comfortable with my body, and yet infinitely scared.

In a way it's always a big surprise to witness people being attracted to me. Perhaps I was more used to it when I was younger, but I believe I was always surprised. I never expected it. Consciousness of my charm is a cumbersome gift. I don't know where to put it or what to do with it—like one too many balls when you try to juggle.

The morning I became aware that Ketut liked me was the morning after the first fever spike. It was the morning when I stayed in bed while everyone else went on a scooter ride along the coast. I remember laying under the bed canopy, not really tired, the back of my neck heavy from restlessness. I remember a ray of sun poking through the blinds. I was feeling lazy and triumphant—a feeling I've always associated with high fever. It is the moment when, confined to bed, I observe with delight the agitation of the outside world: people completing the draining task of carrying themselves around, of doing things, of saying things. That morning I was seeing the rough grain of the bedsheet in the foreground and further out, stuck to the canopy net, a mosquito exhausted pause. I decided to stay there all day, without moving, like the mosquito.

After I made that delectable decision, there was a knock on the door.

I can't be sure whether I said "Come in." Ketut came in with a fancy-looking bottle and stood still behind the canopy.

"Good morning," he said. "They told me you're sick and I brought some miracle water."

The veil of the net made him look like the ghost of a dwarf entering a temple with an offering. I chuckled on the spot.

"It's not funny," he said seriously, and immediately I laughed harder.

He seemed unfazed by my laugh attack, almost satisfied with it, or perhaps just waiting for it to subside, which it didn't. I don't remember how it ended. I must have fallen asleep while laughing—with no transition. I woke up and noticed that the ray of sun had shifted to the other window. Ketut had left the room and placed the bottle on the bedside table. It was the only clue that he had ever been there. I found myself confused and weary and not particularly proud of my behavior. I drank a gulp of the miracle water before collapsing again onto the pillow. And then I remember having this romantic notion that I was never going to leave the island. I would eventually lose my acrylic toenail and would empty myself of my substance through the hole left from the missing nail.

Perhaps this idea of entrapment was born during a visit to one of the temples. Ketut had explained that cremations on this island could take place many years after a person's death. The timing would hinge on the family and clan availability, possessions, and willingness to return the dead to their next life. The dead would be buried and simply laid on the ground pending cremation. That period of time between death and cremation was like taking a break: a restful pause between two lives.

Everyone was scared I'd contracted dengue. We'd have to wait three more days to get testing done and be sure. In the fever I was humming songs from childhood that my sister recognized. The temperature made her clearer to me, or fuzzier, with various layers of likability. She was less the quiet lake I'd always known; she was something else too—something explorable. My head hurt, which made me like her more. She'd wipe my forehead even if I asked her not to. *It's fine*, I'd say, although I wanted her to do this. I think my sister was mirroring the hope of becoming her own souvenir.

In the fourth day after the fever broke, I had a rash best described as islands of white in a sea of red. Testing confirmed dengue. A decision had been made to not take me to a local hospital, which may have made things worse. I was carried along in the minivan, occupying the last row all by myself, laying across the seats, watching flies land on the window's curtains. I didn't see the landscape we moved across; I missed the early-morning hike on the volcano; I missed the waterfalls. From this trip I only got to know the rice fields and the temples; the rest would be a dream from the backseats of a minivan. The itch wasn't terrible, and Ketut was considerate. He brought me little green rice cakes filled with shredded coconut and cane syrup. When I got better I started smoking again—Ketut's cigarettes. Ketut and I sat in the shadow of the minivan and smoked. He mentioned smoking was not well-perceived for women on the island. He said it was expected from women of a certain kind. He didn't ask whether I understood what he meant.

Soon the trip would come to an end. My sister's children had to go back to school. I'd have to stay a bit longer to make sure the fever resolved and the disease wouldn't proceed to anything more critical. There'd be very little chance of that happening and no reason to ask anyone to stay behind. I would take care of myself. Ketut would return to his village near the center of the island. Before leaving, he'd visit me one last time. There would be a pause. A moment when he would appear to be looking for words followed by a moment when he would apologize for his poor English and his poor everything. I wouldn't say anything. I'd offer an elusive smile and ask for a cigarette. When we'd be done smoking, he'd say that the world was no bigger than a leaf.

A few days passed and the fever would rise again. Something else I'd remember and I will recount too. I stayed in a bungalow on the north shore and my bathtub was installed over a pond. From the edge of the tub, I'd dangle a yarn with improvised bait and catch a fish that I'd keep releasing. There'd be a small turtle too, which I would feed; her small mouth would nearly touch my fingers with every bite. Also sitting in the tub, I'd write a long letter to my sister slowly, very slowly, describing precisely the feeling of voluptuous fear that would coil itself in me. I would do this with a lot of care. For what am I if not precise and careful and composed?

What I think is that, in that moment, doing those things on the edge of a tub sitting on a pond, I felt like having a giant and wild fit of laughter that would echo across the pond.

And then later in two weeks, I would come back home— almost thirty-eight and I would come back home, in two weeks, after this vacation, before the month's end. I am thinking it's not funny, and inevitably it makes me laugh.

Immersion

My husband and I first started dynamic apnea as a way to combat our Sundays lulls. It's true we needed a behavioral change—something that would take the edge off those suicidal dominical afternoons. I remember laying it out there on the dining room table between the breadcrumbs and the coffee mugs: it's not like we didn't know it was coming. IT WAS COMING—on the tail of Sunday morning tennis and Sunday morning run—came in that order: boredom, self-observation, emptiness, hopelessness, and an exhausting sense of isolation. I remember my husband commenting that perhaps it was okay, his blue eyes fixed on mine, his right leg in a perpetual shake. He was waiting for me to add or do something. I remember very well not knowing what it was he was waiting for or wondering if he was waiting at all. And so I blacked out: my face like a close-up on a TV quiz show, all my blemishes blown-up and a large-scale dumbness. And then one thing led to the next: I looked up at our TV screen in the corner of the room and saw Dwayne Johnson roaring underwater in the blockbuster about a gigantic earthquake. The TV paused there as if it was too much for the screen to move on.

Dwayne Johnson's open jaw struck me as marvelous. Something relaxed in me at the sight of this colossal, diagonally tilted face. Having a mimetic imagination, I, too, tilted my head sideways. It was a gesture that was perhaps meant as a sign of submissiveness, but I never thought of it that way. In any case, that's when I said it. With my head still tilted, I said to my husband: I'll tell you what, we'll do this: from now on we'll go free diving on Sunday afternoons.

He agreed on the spot. There was no objection, no standoff, no request for time to reflect. I remember him smiling in the void across the dining-room table, carefully assembling the breadcrumbs in one spot and slowly wiping them off the table into his left palm. My husband always cleaned the crumbs this way, using both his hands, without a sponge.

Maybe I can say it like this: my husband and I needed to stop breathing each other's breath. Or maybe I can say it like that: my husband and I always shared one single oxygen tank.

∾

A bit of research led us to a small, local free divers' community and a neighborhood pool with dedicated hours. Dynamic training started pool-based for obvious reasons. It was safe, controlled, warm, and familiar. There was an instructor with an exceedingly common name, which my husband and I kept forgetting. I alternately called him Mike or Bob or John. He was pretty sweet and never took offense or even tried to correct me; perhaps he was relieved by the anonymity. Between us my husband referred to him as G.I. Joe because he was so cut and dried and decent and thin. He projected an unguarded curiosity, a sort of gentle expectation; he'd stop most of his sentences midway, letting the missing half float through the mind of the listener. He didn't have the conventional authority you'd expect in an instructor; his clout derived from the calm openness of people who speak with moderation.

The first phase of the training happened outside of the water, and G.I. Joe started by teaching us warm-up routines. It was implicit from his half-speak that those were mostly meant for thoracic stretching. The more flexible our torso, the more air we'd be able to take in with a maximum breath. Other drills focused on empty-lung stretches, which would allow us to compress at depth and hopefully reduce our residual volume. Each routine didn't have to be long: fifteen to twenty minutes at most. The main thing was to settle our minds before a dive.

My husband and I didn't know much about breathing; this was not something that had required much thought. Breathing had been one more thing that he and I did twenty-four seven. G.I. Joe's routine turned it into something to think about, something that could be improved constantly. You could breathe deep or shallow, hyperventilate or stop.

You could fill up your lungs till they burst or empty them until your thorax would flatten like a crepe. Breathing became this thing my husband and I cared about, this thing that had to be done better: alone and as a couple.

After weeks of practicing the routines, breathing became second nature as well as a major distraction. You could say that conscious breathing saturated this phase of our lives. My husband started commenting on other people's breathing and how it shaped them into who they were; how it really determined their fate. He kept looking for cues in people around him: reporting the number of breaths his boss would take during their weekly meetings; timing the average length of a sigh from one of his colleagues who was prolific with them.

For me it seemed obvious to use apnea as a weapon. I practiced preemptive apnea with obnoxious salespeople in shoe stores or when riding the elevator with neighbors whose faces I didn't like. One day I stopped breathing as one of my cousins commented on the poor shape of our teacups. My husband came into the room at that moment and noticed what I was doing. He joined me in the process. That got us into further and longer experiments. No one around us seemed to notice and I liked that. When someone breathed oddly in our presence, my husband would exhale quietly, as though he was telling me a secret (but loud enough so everyone could hear). In a matter of weeks, breathing and the absence thereof had become code.

I suspected my husband trained more than I did. Both

of us were competitive but he was more. There was an es-
calation in how he approached what had first started as a
hopeless joke.

My husband always had a limitless admiration for top-
level sportsmen and women. Now he had a chance to
physically embrace their culture: training, rigor, work,
persistence, and repetition. He spent more time in
the bathroom than I ever knew him to. He was clearly
training there, taking long baths with the door closed. I
tried eavesdropping but all I got was a breathless quiet.
His training started taking more and more space in the
apartment. Silence and shadows swirled around the plants
on our windowsills. In the beginning I remember feeling
lonely and let down. I regretted having suggested free diving
in the first place. But I never wanted to be a wimp, and so
all I could do was to start seriously training—anywhere, at
any time—until I got better myself. I pushed my limits.

One evening I was practicing empty-lung spells as I was
walking down the stairs with groceries, and I fell flat on my
forehead. I passed out cold and woke up on my husband's
chest, then fell asleep or half asleep, my aching head floating up and down his ribcage. I remember listening to his
low heartbeat as he started to grab me. I tried to stay stuck
to him, to his torso, which wasn't easy. We fought in the
dark, and of course we stopped breathing. It was lovely: the
kind of bittersweet thing that happens between two boxers
as they fall into each other's arms after ten rounds.

After that night trying to find sleep on my husband's

chest became this habit, my head sandwiched between his skin and the bed sheets, holding on to his rhythm. I remember thinking that his heartbeat was the metronome of my downtime. But that would be only partially true: many kinds of beats were part of my night world at the time. Our building sat on a hill overlooking a highway. I don't know how many times I woke up in the middle of the night and stood on the balcony, cutting darkness with my hands (I had quit smoking), listening to the incessant buzz of cars, people coming and going all the time. The night would rise and fall as this giant lung, and I could insert myself in its cavities: hypersmall, unbreathing and unyielding.

Once, before dawn, my unusually perky husband, in his boxer shorts, joined me on the balcony. He carried a book, a flashlight, and a pencil for a new exercise he had devised. He asked me to sit on the floor and make myself comfortable. He instructed me to open the book to a random page and take a deep breath in and hold it: and continue holding as I started reading under the halo of his flashlight. I should keep reading, he said, until I couldn't hold my breath any longer. I had to mark how far down I had read with the pencil. He would keep track of my progress, and he'd mark his own with a different-shaped mark (a small triangle).

I remember he asked for orange juice that same morning and there was none. I remember forgetting to buy orange juice several weeks in a row.

I think it was the same week, or maybe that same day,

that I read about another possible practice on the internet. All that was needed was a sidewalk and a stopwatch. During our morning walk to the train station for work, I instructed my husband to start holding his breath for one minute while standing still. After the minute had passed, I made him start walking down our street at a calm but steady pace, maintaining his breath-hold. He should go as far as he could without breathing.

One day he almost made it all the way to the station.

I remember the day I made it. I had cheated. I was going to say I had cheated, but I hesitated for a second. Then I realized, quite clearly, that no, I didn't want to say it. I started buying orange juice again.

G.I. Joe was surprised by how good both of us were after only three months of practicing the routines. According to him, my husband and I were ready for the pool series.

∽

Pool sessions lasted about an hour, half of it outside and half in the water. G.I. Joe was so thin you could count his ribs. He was constantly cold and his lips would turn purplish five minutes into the lesson. Despite that, he never wore a wetsuit. It was against his religion or so he semi-said.

The pool was relatively small, not Olympic. The locals talked about a mega pool that was in the works. It was like they were talking about a dream. I never could find out whether they were making this up. To be honest, I never tried. Size didn't matter. At least not in the beginning.

Initially we went every Sunday for group sessions, but then we started going weekdays in the evening as we found out that G.I. Joe was trying to round-up figures by offering privates.

⌢

I knew my body wasn't ready for the blind swim. I knew it as soon as I saw the roll of duct tape on the diving block. Something in me didn't agree with duct tape. I was ready to give up breathing but not seeing. I said nothing. I decided that keeping quiet and letting my husband go first was a very effective way to buy time.

I had begun to figure out that my husband could do things I wasn't ready to do myself, and the annoyance of that thought fueled whatever part in me wasn't a chicken. Even though I did everything I could to repress my irritation, the idea of not keeping up with him had become, for me, the most devastating thing imaginable. "Please go," I said when he asked.

I watched G.I. Joe cover my husband's mask with strips of duct tape so he couldn't see through it at all. G.I. Joe was very methodical, and the duct tape was silver and textured like a sheet of coarse fabric. "Fancy duct tape," I said stupidly, and I remember that, in that moment, something dark and sexual soared in the back of my mind.

Under G.I. Joe's instructions, I guided and accompanied my blind-masked husband into the pool. I took him to the side and placed his hands onto the wall right under the surface of the water. After taking a deep breath, he dove under the surface and started swimming slowly down the side of the pool, guiding himself only by touch. I was instructed to dive with him, to be his apnea-mate, watching underwater and swimming along. I remember the feeling of being swallowed by the water, trying to be absent from myself, to almost fall asleep, to imagine my blind husband as a dream.

During the first pool length without breathing, I made myself as empty as possible. I tried to not think at all. Thoughts appeared, of course, but I didn't hold on to them; I let them slide through me and dissolve in the water like sugar cubes. I don't remember what the thoughts were, just that they were very soluble. Totally empty, I'd consume a minimum of energy and oxygen. I remember feeling like a standby screen with the eye of a micro-camera pointed at my husband. Someone was shouting up above. G.I. Joe's encouragements got through to us like wet whales' songs.

My diaphragm began contracting toward the end of the third pool length; the spasms started as my husband initiated his third turn. From then on I knew they'd become more intense and closer together. I was entering the fighting phase. There was no cheating in the pool. There was no out. There was only my husband, swimming slowly along the wall. I remember thinking that if he did, then perhaps I could hold a little longer. Perhaps I closed my eyes.

Next I remember my husband lifting me out of the water, holding me in his arms like an oversized baby. I remember the warm, rubbery texture of his short fingers on my ribcage. I remember thinking of something terrible and forgetting immediately.

∽

One year after my husband and I started free diving, the group organized a trip to a miniature and southerly island off the coast. It was a small and intimate outing headed by G.I. Joe. The water was warm and the skies were clear. There was a twenty-meter line to follow for the dives—a standard beginners' length; G.I. Joe wanted us to take a few of them for fun. My husband and I hadn't exactly become pro divers by then, but each of us had sufficient diving experience to be invited on that excursion.

That afternoon G.I. Joe accompanied us on each dive and took some on his own to unknown depths. He failed to resurface on his third dive. The group didn't panic right away; there was a rather slow-building anxiety that developed to a climax as the timer kept ticking.

My husband dove to look for him and I followed. There was this moment when the two of us were at the bottom of the rope, looking. The water was very clear, and there was no sign of life anywhere: no fish, no G.I. Joe. There was nothing but the textured ceiling of the water surface and the fragmented light that came through it. My husband and I waited, immobile, with our arms down by our sides and our hands half opened. My husband's wetsuit looked ash-blue underwater, like the skin of a marine mammal re-upholstered on a human shape. The fear that I had felt on the surface was different down there: thicker and sharp-er, compressed by the water density and the absence of oxygen. I remember when the quietude hit us, when my husband and I knew for sure that G.I. Joe was lost. And that's when I stopped looking and thinking that he would inevitably show up somewhere underneath us, swimming upward like a ghost jellyfish.

I decided to quit; at that very moment, I stopped want-ing to dive. I suppose that's also when my husband's aspira-tions began to be quashed. He and I never had, in any case, long, nightly discussions about what had happened; maybe because that was when the desire for babies arrived.

Ten months later I was pregnant. Our apartment was big-ger and had a freestanding bathtub with lion's feet. Every once in a while, I soaked in it, or I just sat in it, empty, and got lost watching my naked belly grow. I worshipped that bathtub. I scrubbed it clean after each use; I remember wanting it spotless. I had a premonitory religious fervor for that tub.

∽

The day it happened, I watched a wet spot spreading underneath me on the couch like an island in formation. Perhaps I had a moment between contractions where I could actually think like that—about islands being formed.

My husband was out shopping. I moaned on the telephone. He said to wait for him. I moaned again. Some instinct pushed me in the bathtub and made me turn the water on full throttle. I waited for my husband.

At some point I put my head underwater.

I decided to wait until I could not wait any longer.

I remember thinking that this was going to be the most romantic moment of my life.

The Door Test

Between them is a door. Not too intimidating but still a door. Narrow: about two and a quarter by seven feet in size; all wood—solid red oak, or a good imitation. It is the thickest and strongest door in Lucille's apartment; resistant to warping. If one didn't know better, this could be the entry door, intended to act as a shield from external intrusion, immune to termite attacks—the type made workable for years by an independent artisan in a small workshop in the countryside. Using her imagination and more time to think, Lucille could smell the scent of the wood chips and the artisan sweat as the door was born. But right now Lucille cannot indulge in that sort of reverie, because she's having a conversation with her grandmother. She is sitting on one side of the door (the outside) and Celeste—the grandmother—on the other (the inside). To be clear: the door leads to the bathroom, and there is only one bathroom in Lucille's apartment. Tonight Celeste is locked in that bathroom and she remains invisible, although until now she's done most of the talking.

Lucille can only think of very few instances in which people are having conversations across a closed door: a confession to a Catholic priest, a parley in a jail visiting ward, withdrawing money from an old-fashioned bank teller, a secret family reunion across the former Berlin Wall. In all of the above, there is always a device to break the closure: a grid or lattice, a fully tempered glass, a hole. But in their case, there is no such device—just a simple and honest closed door.

It is 6:00 p.m. now, and by that time on most nights, Lucille is setting the dinner table using Celeste's wedding silverware. A few feet away in the living room, Celeste is watching *Nexus* on Channel 5. *Nexus* is a TV game where each candidate is teamed with a celebrity. Each contestant has to make the celebrity find a particular word, by providing seven one-word clues within ninety seconds. Every now and then Lucille steps out of the kitchen and stands behind her grandmother's recliner. Enticed by each other's presence, they both shout words as they think of them— usually much faster than the celebrities, who tend to have pea-sized brains. On occasion, Celeste or Lucille throws a projectile at the TV screen in frustration—usually a magazine; sometimes reading glasses. The shouting and throwing is at the heart of their intimacy; it is a shared moment, light and important. Sometimes they disagree over a word, and only one of them is proved right by the commentator. When the screen turns black for the credits, they move to the kitchen, where they have their candlelit dinner. The usual ending to those evenings is a small glass of port or a shot of aged tequila; by then the small pillar candles are burning out. Then Lucille cleans the dishes while Celeste brushes what's left of her teeth and plops her dentures in a glass. When this is done, Lucille walks her grandmother to her bed and tucks her in. After a good eight-hour sleep, they wake up to the next day.

But this is an unusual evening, at least for now. The TV is turned off, and Celeste is locked in the bathroom; it is unclear how long it will take to get her out of there. When she gets out, the story will end. As long as she's caged, the story will move forward. The story will go on until Celeste opens the door, or Lucille breaks down the door.

This blind face-to-face is starting to take its toll on Lucille. Maybe the velvet stool on which she's sitting lacks an armrest. She throws questions like an amateur, with no particular expectation:

"Did you really push down as you were turning the knob? Did you take off your compression stockings? You know you shouldn't, right? Why did you lock the door anyway? Do you realize what time it is? What the hell is the locksmith doing?"

From behind the door, Celeste's voice comes back smoky and resolute, honoring each question in the order it was received: "I pushed and turned. My compression stockings are torn, and you forgot to buy me new ones. I need my privacy just like anyone else. It is 6:45 p.m. and the locksmith is probably having dinner. Don't get too excited. Why don't you make yourself a cup of tea?"

∾

Lucille fixes herself a cup of tea, satisfied to carry out a simple manual task. She tends to internalize everything like a Crock-Pot: the sound of water boiling, the smell of jasmine leaves, the cling of a spoon, the silence of sugar crystals. It's a habit of hers; she locks everything in and processes. Perhaps she's a very inert woman who cannot escape her own digestion. Perhaps the speed of light is different in her world, slower, and her time is messed up. She knows not to adjust. She's locked in herself and her grandmother is locked in the bathroom.

Celeste is not really Lucille's grandmother, but it is hard for Lucille not to think of her that way. Celeste is just her grandfather's widow, and Lucille says "grandmother" because "grandma" would sound too familiar. When she first asked Celeste to come and live with her, there was hesitation. Celeste's acceptance came a few days later in the form of a weird declaration to Lucille's parents: "Lucille is an old maid and she's probably sapphic, but she's well educated." The parents didn't contradict and looked down humbly. This made them look like jurors during the reading of a sentence: Celeste's coming into their daughter's life was indispensable—like the sunrise. As the years passed, Lucille's barren apartment got filled with polished furniture and sophisticated books. This culminated with Celeste's termination of the lease on her storage unit.

Lucille takes good care of the furniture and artifacts. She

displays particular zeal in the dusting of a set of exquisite Russian dolls with round, lunar faces and golden *sarafans*.

∽

Lucille sneaks back to the bathroom door and tries not to make a sound. She wants to spy on Celeste, although spying is a big word for someone invisible. She tries to catch a sigh, a small move, a knee jerk, drops of urine into the bowl. Celeste is dead silent now. Lucille places her left eye on the keyhole. What she sees is a speck of light. It is bright and borderline abstract. It's annoying, like white abstract painting. Lucille doesn't see shit.

"I don't see shit."

"Well, what did you expect?"

"You scared me."

"You spied on me."

"I'm so tired of this."

Actually, Lucille is lying, because she's not tired at all. She's secretly starting to enjoy this moment and hopes that the locksmith won't show up for a while. Across a closed bathroom door, one can have conversations that would be unnatural in a different setting. Lucille suspects that her grandmother messed with the doorknob deliberately. This may be true. It also may be that Lucille projects her own rumination onto her grandmother. Lucille sits down again, satisfied with the sight of the door. She imagines that separation enhances intimacy and closes her eyes.

With her, it's automatic: she reads a good line and closes her eyes until the words become fossils embedded inside her; she makes love and closes her eyes until the warmth of her partner becomes encrusted inside her. This is Lucille's trick to capture bits of otherness.

With her legs stretched out from the stool and her eyes still closed, Lucille starts talking about the project of a trip to Patagonia. It would have to be a cruise, because Celeste is too old to walk. Of course, modern cruises are a bit stupid but they're also casually retro. This one would take really long, because Patagonia is not exactly next door. On the deck they would sit on the loungers and watch the glaciers. Polite waiters would serve tea, and musicians would be too shy to approach them. They would have separate, neighboring cabins, and Lucille would knock on the wall to signal curfew or wake-up time. One of the better-looking musicians (probably a violinist) would eventually bring himself to declare his flame to Lucille, and she would have to turn him down. Celeste would take tons of pictures of Lucille, but she wouldn't let herself be in any shot. Lucille would look like Marlene Dietrich, which is another way of saying that she would look like a thinner, younger version of Celeste.

In fact, Lucille is smaller than her grandmother, and obviously much younger. Her body is slender, where Celeste is plump. Lucille's hands are chapped and wide, her feet unattended; Celeste's extremities are impeccable, like good punctuation. Lucille's eyes are violet and wide-open—she tends to get startled easily; her grandmother's eyes are yellow and slanted, like those of a wrinkled snow leopard. Despite those striking differences, and as is customary for people who have long lived under the same roof, Lucille is starting to look like Celeste. The mailman makes passing compliments about the goodness of their genes—of which they have none in common. This is where the story gets confusing, like the visual experience of standing between two mirrors and seeing the infinite reproduction of one's self.

On the wall in the hallway next to Lucille, there's a picture of Celeste in her late thirties. Lucille has stopped talking and opened her eyes again. She's confronted with the picture. Young Celeste stares at her from under a slanted hat; her bun hangs low on her neck like a pomegranate. It is a glamorous picture, a shot that could only have been taken in the mid-1940s. Lucille has seen this picture a million times, yet tonight the picture gets to be disturbing. Perhaps it is disturbing to talk to a glamorous woman locked in a bathroom. Perhaps it is disturbing to associate a glamorous woman to a sandpaper-and-whisky voice that makes the bathroom door vibrate. Perhaps Lucille is jealous and all she wants is to be like Celeste in that one picture. That is what she wants to be, to become, when she's old: a woman once glamorous in a picture.

"Hi. Good evening," Lucille's inner voice says. "I once was glamorous. I was the most glamorous of all."

"You're looking at the picture," Celeste says.

"No."

"You like the glamour of it. You'd like to be glamorous."

"No."

"What would you like to be?"

"Well, I don't like that question," Lucille retorts. "What if I asked you now?"

"I would like to be on a cruise to Patagonia."

The door has moved again, and Lucille shivers from the cold or motionlessness or from what Celeste just said. She encapsulates them: the door and Celeste behind it, both of them trailing along her fantasies. She pictures the door as a ventricle, collecting Celeste's sounds and expelling them toward her. The door is pumping. That's the door's job.

Lucille looks at her watch and reconsiders a possibility that she has earlier thoroughly repressed: Celeste has not gotten her insulin today, and her condition will worsen if she stays stuck much longer. Right now it is possible that Celeste is committing assisted suicide. Bewildered from the thought, Lucille tries to distract herself by coming up with different scenarios to end the story right:

The locksmith shows up and opens the bathroom door with a hairpin, like a gentleman burglar. Celeste gets out and Lucille gets married.

The locksmith shows up and breaks the door down with a single shoulder strike. A mystified Celeste is found standing on the geriatric toilet seat. Lucille and the locksmith burst into fits of loud and coarse laughter.

The locksmith doesn't show up, and Celeste gets bored

and gets out. The locksmith comes in after the fact and Lucille gets engaged.

The locksmith doesn't show up, and Lucille pounds the area below the doorknob with a brick. The locksmith doesn't show up, ever.

Perhaps Lucille is exaggerating, as always. Celeste's diabetes is not so severe, and in time she will get out of the bathroom. After all, the worst possible ending would be a long night of muted conversations ending with a climactic silence, and Celeste's corpse found in the morning as Lucille finally manages to open the door. In movies, corpses are always found at dawn under a bleak, diagonal light. Luckily, this is not a movie.

The story moves on, if only to comply with the ludicrous mandate: Celeste is locked up. For the time being there are no wide angles, no offstage commentary, no incidental music, only one idea that crawls perniciously in Lucille's brain. The idea is so vivid that Lucille could point on her head to the precise spot where it resides: somewhere behind her right ear. Lucille scratches the spot but the idea only gets bolder—as if some shady surgeon had implanted a magnet in her skull, and all of Lucille's reflections line up with it. The concept, which started wordless, grows into one single short sentence: "I can think with Celeste's head." Lucille repeats it silently, as if under a spell: "Hi, I can think with my grandmother's head."

In Celeste's head, Lucille's gaze runs serenely over the dark blue wallpaper inside the cubicle. On one of the walls, there is a floor-to-ceiling bookcase. This makes the room look higher than it is—more dignified. Celeste's skin on her hands is somewhat green, but Lucille can experience the sharpness of her grandmother's amber-colored eyes. Every once in a while, Celeste blinks, and Lucille sees the outer world getting covered with thick eyelids that have imprinted the memory of light.

In Celeste's head, Lucille moves her feet from toes to heel, so she can vary the point of contact with the tile-covered ground. Celeste is nearly always barefoot, and the skin of her soles is, oddly, very soft. Lucille can now taste the softness from the inside. She can see how it allows Celeste to feel the ground underneath the surface. Thinking that way, Lucille undergoes a lower gravity and a sudden hatred for compression stockings.

Inside Celeste, life's circles are tighter, and the temporary lockup in the bathroom feels like just one more circle. There's no anxiety and no expectation, just a smaller space that can only contain the present and a few memories. Even the memories get kicked out by the present; one can tell, because they're different by the minute. There's only one persistent reality: the reality of Lucille's invasive feelings.

Lucille realizes that her feelings for Celeste are slightly condescending, and it bothers her a lot. She can only pretend they're on equal footing. At times that pretense can be farcical, like when she tried and failed to fit Celeste, in her wheelchair, onto the building's elevator. Celeste never complains, which makes things worse. Right now Celeste has been locked up for four hours and she hasn't protested once.

Lucille doesn't like the silence behind the closed bathroom door, and she worries about the insulin again. She worries and listens: a period of hyped unwellness settles. She can't deny that part of her enjoys the drama, and in that, indeed, she thinks with Celeste's head. It's not cruelty, not even morbid curiosity. It's a kind of exuberance; a spark of vitality poured over her as she sits in waiting and wonders again and again: "Are you thinking what I'm thinking?" Lucille knows that, sooner or later, Celeste will walk through the door. She imagines herself relieved, then upset and, in the end, massively peaceful. It's fine: this is how it is. One thinks someone else's thoughts through a closed door in order to get the door open, or ends up dying alone in someone else's head. It is that moment. That awkward moment of impossible tenderness.

Full of Grace

It was the fall of 1985, just a few weeks after my husband and I had moved to Pasadena, California, all the way from our native Nantes. We were to spend the next three years there, as Michel had been appointed at Caltech to teach differential equations to the undergrads.

What Michel called his "equadiffs" would always be a complete mystery to me, although he had made several attempts to make proper introductions. He would point at the colorful graphs in his office, and I would watch with unlearned deference; fine, colored wrinkles beyond question, red and blue elegant intertwining lines with flowing names such as "Traveling waves and shocks," "Energy in System," "Veloc-force."

Pasadena would be a shock wave indeed, and what had first sounded to me like the name of a Latin dance or a Brazilian seashore was in those early days the promise of even more. I couldn't quite grasp the brightness of the place. Pasadena had sunlight so pervasive that no shade in the house could temper it. I had to lead a life with sunglasses, inside and out; weeks of uninterrupted sun. Of course, I had the nights to recover, nights with a quality of air as light and breezy as chocolate mousse. We slept naked.

By October, I was in my eighth month and big as a cruise liner. My swollen breasts were leading the way over an abdomen so stiff I expected the skin to burst anytime despite the daily use of lotion. My curvy rear end was at the stern of a body that had overgrown me beyond belief, and I kept touching the different parts of my anatomy like a dreamer trying to pinch herself back to reality. I was thirty-nine and pregnant for the first time.

Every morning, Michel would leave at dawn and kiss me on the small protuberant hook-bone at the nape of my neck. Under no circumstances would I miss the ritual even if my compressed bladder threatened a second Hiroshima: kiss first, bathroom next.

After he'd left, I'd wake up hungry as an ogress and walk to the diner down the block for the full American breakfast experience. The place was warm and woody, with square marble tables and fresh-cut flowers. There awaited worn metal teapots, silky egg yolks slightly veiled, soaked teabags on porcelain, handwritten menus on white boards; all different angles of the Promised Land. An ancient TV set was posted in a corner—always on. Tradition *oblige*.

The diner keeper was an old-fashioned beauty who reminded me of Irene Dunne in *Love Affair*. Her smile radiated like an Icelandic fireplace, and every now and then she'd ask: "So when are you due again, honey?"

It was one of those Indian summer mornings, and I was drowning crispy warm bread in my Benedicts while trying to read *Time* magazine and occasionally lifting my head to watch the news. The boy had been sitting catty-corner to me under one of the windows. I watched him whenever I felt he wouldn't notice. He had a pack of Lucky Strikes next to a large foamy cup of coffee, but more interestingly he wore the white collar of a Roman Catholic priest. With the milky skin of a redhead, albeit no trace of red in his washed blond hair, the boy looked terribly young. A youth incompatible with priesthood, I decided.

"You don't look like you're from around here," he said from across the room, obviously noticing I had been watching.

"Probably because I'm not," I responded.

That morning, we had the diner all to ourselves, and the three of us must have formed an odd triangle of a kind: the child priest, the Icelandic beauty, and me—the overgrown mother-to-be. It created a strange atmospheric imbalance, almost imperceptible, like the gravity of an ever-so-slightly slanted plane where marbles are put in slow motion. I stood up and strode between the tables toward the boy, a gush of motherly hormones giving me sudden confidence.

"Hi, I'm Hélène and there's no hiding I'm from France. What's your name?" I asked.

He stood up too quickly, almost kicking his chair to the floor in the process. He wasn't wearing a full robe, just a black collarino and matching black pants, both floating a little on a thin frame. The Church hadn't yet covered his body in full; the boy was still permitted a bit of manliness.

"Hi. Thomas," he said.

He raised a hand in a begging gesture for me to catch it, and we shook hands like strangers are supposed to do on a first meet. It was a peculiar motion, exclusive, which made the diner and the Icelandic waitress lose color. Although it lasted only seconds, the focus was so intense that I felt like a child myself, my head tilted over a difficult drawing in progress, my tongue stuck from the corner of my mouth. We weren't looking at each other; we were looking at our hands as if they were detached from us.

"Do you mind?" I said, gesturing to the chair across from him.

"Oh please, by all means!" he said and grabbed the back of the chair to make room, then placed it gently under me as I sat. I always liked the rules of etiquette—in that moment, the boy had marked ten points right off the bat.

"Are you from Pasadena yourself, Thomas?"

"No, I came here to study," he said. "Besides, very few are true Pasadenian. The last of the natives must have left in the first half of the nineteenth century."

"Interesting you would say that . . ." I whispered.

"You mean interesting that an American would make any historical reference at all?" he said abruptly.

I paused and observed him, not gratifying him with a response that would have been either untruthful or would appear so in any case. I was growing curious of this mixture of shy politeness and awkward passion.

His face had moved forward over his neck, which now exhibited a web of tendons and veins framing the protruding Adam's apple. His eyes had opened up, and their color was as puzzling as the boy himself—a paragon of in-between: a greenish brown gleaming toward blue under the direct light flowing from the window.

I had decided to let the boy reflect on his question and how he had thrown it at me from a slingshot of his soul. Soul was, after all, the groundwork from which he had chosen to elevate his career, and it was fair that his question would fire right back. The silence was deliciously awkward.

"I don't know why I said that," he said now in a low voice, a red surge flowing from the white rectangle of his collar straight up to the cheekbones. There was some firework under his skin.

I started laughing, one of those deep and honest laughs that rose from below the lungs. It was uncontrollable, like a hiccup, an irritation of the nerves that kept building itself up to an apogee. This wasn't a discreet chuckle—nothing Anglo-Saxon about it. It was pure Latin guttural hysteria, which fired across the room and ricocheted against the walls.

I overpowered him and it didn't take long for him to join me. The boy had guts. He kept pulling at his Catholic collar while his eyes had disappeared under an array of solar wrinkles. I liked that.

"It's good to laugh," I said at last while leaning back in my chair and grabbing my oversized girth with both hands.

"It is," the boy said and wiped what looked like tears on either side of his eyes. "May I say something?" he added.

"Anything except asking for permission to say it," I said.

"You make an iconic pregnant lady." He paused. "What I mean to say . . ." His face and neck were red again. He could not utter the words.

I was both startled and flattered by this inconsequential flirt, liberated because of my pregnancy, liberated because of his faith. We both had good excuses. The young man had managed to confuse himself as to who we were: a man and a woman in a diner making conversation for the first time. I had no desire to help him out. I looked at him in the eyes.

He started again. "You see," he said, "you look just like the image of pregnancy."

"Aha. And how could this be iconic? Some people consider my condition embarrassing and improper to look at. The pregnant woman belongs in her home and not in some nice and cozy diner."

Thomas was looking at his fingers now. I could tell the Icelandic beauty was listening in from behind the bar, wiping wineglasses that were sparkling and dry already.

"Do you come here often, Thomas? I don't think I've seen you before."

"I usually stay and eat at the seminary. I had the day off and wandered about. It's a long walk from there." The redness in his face was starting to fade as he toyed with his pack of Luckies.

"You can smoke if you want to. I really wouldn't mind; I might even appreciate it. I haven't smoked in ages."

"But you shouldn't and so I shouldn't."

"Wisely spoken." I smiled and realized I must have been smiling the whole time. I felt vibrant, like a purring cat.

"So how long do you have to go before ordination?"

"I'm in the second year of my Master of Divinity. I still have awhile to go." He stopped. "Look . . ." he started, "I apologize for what I said earlier. It wasn't appropriate. About the pregnancy . . . I spend so much time in the seminary, I forget how to be in the world. Please forget it."

"I will," I said.

He got up to leave. "I'd better head back. It's getting late and I have to study."

"I'll treat you to your coffee," I said. "No strings attached. You go and study." I waved a dismissive hand sweep.

"Okay," he said. "Thank you very much."

Thomas had spoken like a car that wouldn't start, with lots of pauses and an ignition that failed to do the trick. He went out and I watched him walk behind the diner's window in the splashing sunlight. In one of the top corners, a flock of pigeons flew by. When the Icelandic beauty gave me my change back, I could read cold judgment in her eyes. I had scored low with her that morning, and I felt the need to tip big.

The following evening, while chatting with Michel, I talked about my morning encounter. Somehow, in the tell-

ing, I must have seemed protective of Thomas, as if antici-
pating some anti-clerical remark from Michel—defending
a faith and a clergy that I had rejected throughout the first
half of my life. I found myself praising Thomas's vocation-
al impulse and his courage in carrying on with it.

"Vocation . . ." He paused. "What did he look like?"

"Who?"

"Who do you think? The priest-to-be, the guy from the
diner of course!"

"Oh, Michel . . . And how does this have anything to do
with anything?"

"Everything. It has everything to do with everything."

"Well, good, I suppose. In an odd kind of way."

"I thought so. Vocation would only take you so far."

"Thanks, Michel. It's great that you see such depth in me,
in my behavior out in the world, especially when I'm eight
months along."

"So what? You wouldn't flirt because you're pregnant? Is
that what you want me to believe? You look dangerously
good, Hélène, especially now." A sinuous smile was swimming across Michel's face.

"Oh, please . . ." I stiffened as I stood in front of him.

"Oh, please . . ." he repeated as he was closing in on me,
his hands landing on my outstretched skin.

"Flirt with me," he ordered.

∿

That night, I couldn't fall asleep. I kept trying to convince myself that I was getting some rest by just lying in bed; that, at some point, my mind would grow weary of my body. There were too many obstacles. My pregnant body was one, which at this point only permitted one specific side position with a pillow stuffed between my thighs. My mind was another, racing along Michel's light snoring, racing along his hands on me, racing along Thomas's cloudless face when he laughed.

At around 2:00 a.m., I got up and went into the kitchen to drink a glass of water. I filled the glass from the refrigerator's dispenser, and in the dark, some water must have spilled and formed a small puddle. As I stepped away from the fridge, my bare feet got wet. For a second I believed my water had broken, and I checked myself, but there was nothing.

I went onto the terrace to breathe some air—softer than any I had breathed that year. In the corner of the night, I listened to the sound of freight trains and isolated cars—manmade machines that were heading somewhere. "Give me your ears," the machines were saying. "God says for me to tell you that all of you must report here if they want to deliver." The Pasadena night had become a giant delivery room.

∾

Over the next three days, I pretended to have forgotten about Thomas.

I stayed home for the most part and procrastinated and looked out the seventeen windows of our house.

At some point, I started packing for the hospital. This was the one thing that all guidebooks about pregnancy agreed upon: pack your belongings so that you are ready when it comes. For some reason, I couldn't comprehend the instructions and kept undoing and redoing the same tasks.

Most books suggested packing two different bags: one for what was needed during labor and another for what wouldn't be needed until after giving birth. I found it confusing. I placed two nightgowns in the same bag despite repeated advice to keep one for before and a fresh one for after. In the end and when I was done with it, I lifted one bag with each hand and figured the labor bag was much lighter than the afterbirth bag.

On the fourth day I decided to spend the morning reading the *Pasadena Star-News* through and through. At the end of the local cultural section, my eyes got caught by a tiny column. The font was so small that I had to get Michel's reading glasses to decipher. It read:

> On November 2, Rev. Tobias E. will be celebrating a solemn requiem mass for All Souls' Day at St. Andrew's Catholic Church. Joseph P. and Thomas F. from the Fuller Theological Seminary will serve mass for this special event. The choir of Holy Family

will perform. This traditional mass is anticipated with much ex-
citement from all the members of Pasadena's Catholic community.

When Michel came back from work late that afternoon,
he blew the door open and caught me by surprise as I was
coming down the stairs. For a second, I felt guilty. His coat
still on, he announced that some hotshot from Caltech
wanted him to contribute to an upcoming publication in a
prestigious mathematical review. This was major.

"There's one serious downside," he pursued.

"Which is?"

"I have to attend a conference in Oxford the first week of
November."

"And?"

"And you're due on November 12."

"Right. Right . . . but you'll surely be back by then."

"What if I'm not? What if you go into labor early?"

"What if you don't go? What if you don't write your article? What if your career goes down the drain due to bad
timing? There's no debate here. I can manage on this end."

"I'll think about it."

"Think about it then," I threatened, knowing full well
that he had decided to go.

He took me out for a walk that night. It was hazy outside
and the streetlights created an oblique and sepia halo under the oak trees, as if the two of us were strolling along
the entrails of the city. The streets were empty and Michel

must have decided to ignore the sidewalks to lead us onto the middle of the road, where the echo of our steps was louder. We walked under the realization that no place in Europe would ever offer such carnal eeriness. As we got back home, I felt as though my skin was covered in a very fine maternal dew.

"Do you feel happy here?" he asked as I was fumbling for the key inside my purse.

"Oh, yes! I like the air, I like the light. It's very beautiful."

"I'm not asking about the weather, Hélène. I know you're pretty isolated here. In Nantes, we had friends, dinner parties, heated conversations. Do you miss all that?"

"I do and I don't. I mean, I know it's temporary. I think I'm getting used to my own company. I ponder a lot over a lot—like a mirror. It's a good thing."

"Maybe. I'd like to spend more time with you. You've changed. Not in a bad way. You're radiant, radioactive. I didn't know you that way. I need more time with you, and soon we'll have less."

"Hurry then! Get to know the new me." I held his wrists and placed his hands over my breasts like a puppeteer, a way of ending a conversation. I wasn't ready to talk.

∾

November 2 that year was a Saturday, and Michel had been in England for two days. He would not return until the following Wednesday.

I had been sitting one hour in front of my closet, debating what to wear, and had settled for a black dress that my body overfilled. My body overfilled everything; my personal space bubble had inflated like an expanding universe, leaving no room for anyone or anything. The expansion had been slow in the first few months of the pregnancy, but in the last weeks, I had felt the speeding spell of some dark energy. My body had become phenomenal; the lightest breeze would spark an explosion of voracity. I was ripe as the ripest fruit, craving thick juices.

I took public transportation to get to St. Andrew's. Although the buzz from the bus was mellow between stations, each stop was abrupt, and I felt the need to hold my belly as if it would make a difference. A man had left me his seat when I first came on board; his eyes had lingered on me a bit too long. I extracted a book from my purse and pretended to be reading.

The ride took about half an hour, and I kept reading the same page over and over with no patience for the words. When the bus reached the St. Andrew's stop, the driver slammed on the brakes, and I was catapulted to the exit. An older black woman grabbed me by the arm to prevent my fall and cursed the driver, calling him a child-murderer. An argument between them ensued, but the doors closed behind me, and the bus went on its way. For a few minutes, I stood there on the street, stunned by my own nerve for having crossed town to come this way. And then, as scattered groups of people were walking in the direction of the church and I was alone, leaning on the glass wall of the bus stop, Thomas reappeared.

"Good to see you here. Will you attend the service?"

I looked up. "How are you?"

"Fine," he said. "I will be serving mass today. It is a special service, you know. You should attend if you can—unless you have other plans."

"I have every intention to go. I came on the bus and nearly got killed—my own Way of Sorrows." I smiled.

"I'm sorry to hear that. Why don't I accompany you to the last station then? I'll find you a good seat." He smiled—a shy, sweet and sour smile, as though he and I had a long-standing history that drew its strength from shared danger and late dinner conversations.

At first, the ostensible closeness repelled me, and I walked maintaining a fair distance between us, and then the distaste melted into a general sense of uneasiness at the thought of the pair of us: a young man in a white robe and a very pregnant woman in a black fitted dress. Yet something was making me walk further, on my own tightrope, as though each step was eating up the last of my pride. Thomas had altered his pace to match my own, and I felt disproportionate relief as we entered the church.

Inside, the silence and the sight of the water font plunged down into a part of myself that I had long disowned. Thomas dipped the tips of his fingers into the water and then turned around to touch my own fingers with his. He did this without passion. His gesture was quick and unaffected: the automatic repetition of a ritual that had become a mindless part of him.

I crossed myself and rehearsed mentally the words I didn't know I still had. "In the name of the Father, and the Son, and the Holy Ghost."

I took a seat in the third row, where Thomas had led me to, before he disappeared behind a side door next to the altar. There were fifteen minutes to go before mass, leaving me ample time to digest what was happening.

The Roman arches and the rose window brought recollections of a childhood I had buried deep beneath the years of happy marriage with Michel and the less happy years of longing for a child who wouldn't come. The child had come at last, and now I had followed a man of the cloth into a church, a man who was too young to be called a man.

The baby was kicking hard to prevent me from indulging in my reverie. I stroked my stomach back and forth and shushed. The child stopped kicking and fell asleep. With the meditation forced upon me by the circumstance, I acknowledged the awakening of another child; a pitiless child I had shut off in a black closet of my conscience. I mothered a growing desire, and the same desire mothered me.

Soon the doors to the church were closed, and the priest walked in from where Thomas had vanished earlier. Thomas and another boy followed and posted themselves on one side of the altar with their backs to us. I glanced at Thomas's neck and then made myself look at the priest.

He had a pedantic voice, which invited us into a period of silence for personal prayers in the stillness of our hearts.

Silence was then broken and the priest started reading:

"Then I heard a voice from heaven say, 'Write: Blessed are the dead who die in the Lord from now on.' 'Yes,' says the Spirit, 'they will rest from their labor, for their deeds will follow them.'"

His sermon went on, and he commented on the various reads of the apocalypse and soon lost me in the sameness of his tone. My eyes had adjusted to the dimly lit space, and I noticed a statue of the Virgin not too far from me with her palms offered and her eyes shut. I watched Thomas again, and I thought he was watching me watching, but he looked down and coughed in his fist, and I couldn't be sure. I willed him to watch me again, but he wouldn't.

What was his intention in all of this? Would he risk something with me? What was something in a priest-to-be's mind? Had he decided never to attempt anything as a natural consequence of his vows? Did he feel pleasure from the traction of his vetoes? I was troubled, but only for a few minutes—that is, until I realized that, a few feet away from me and before the statue of Mary, a votive candle had fallen, and a flame was spreading.

Before long, someone in the back screamed, and it collided rather comically with the monotonous sermon. People stood and started to run toward the exits, while the priest tried to call for calm; Thomas and his acolyte had been there at once and were laboring to put out the fire using the drapery that had covered the front of the altar. This proved insufficient, and as the flames threatened to poke through the drapery again, Thomas took his robe off and used it to cover the last of the burning. His body shone under the lanterns. Maybe he looked back from above his shoulder as I walked out.

Half an hour later, I was sitting on a bench just outside the church next to a fountain. A fire truck was still parked in the front, but the incident had been contained with no real damage or injury. I saw Thomas headed across the street. He now wore a tight V-neck T-shirt and a pair of khakis that could not be his.

On instinct, he turned his head and crossed back toward me.

"I'm sorry. When I said it was going to be a special service, this is not what I intended. I hope you're okay."

"We're just fine. We survived, once again. How about you?"

"No harm done. I'll just have to grow new eyelashes and get a new robe."

I noticed the tips of his lashes were burnt.

"I'm glad. Maybe we should meet in some neutral territory next time: not my diner, not your church. What do you think?" I rubbed my lower back as I spoke, which made my stomach protrude even more.

"I think that's right . . . right," he said with an empty stare above my head.

"I'll tell you what: Here's my address and phone number. We can have coffee if you feel like it. Do it soon though. In my condition this invitation expires before long."

Thomas took the piece of paper I was handing him.

"Merci," he said before he was gone.

This last word touched me more than it had to. I thought about its homophone in English and wondered if I was still capable of mercy, if some part of me would stop what the other had started. It was a fleeting thought, soon buried under the effort of carrying my own weight as I walked back to the bus heading home.

That afternoon, I drank three large cups of watery decaf and busied myself without spirit around the baby's room. At twilight, I sat on the velvet-covered rocker and tried to look at what Thomas had stirred in me and what I intended to do with it. I began to wonder how much more tension my body would endure—a tension that I knew I had created and nurtured. I nourished half-baked hopes: hopes for my desire to be transmissible like a disease; hopes for contact beneath my cracking skin; hopes for freedom, which included freeing myself from the child I carried. What mother would I be if inhabited by this sad madness? Would my hopes pass through the placenta? Did the baby know about me like an inmate would know about his jailer? Who was I, then, to attempt seducing Thomas on a whim? A soon-to-be old woman in search of reassurance? Out of the recollections of my childhood that my visit to the church had triggered, I heard my own mother humming in my ear: "You have the name of a great lover." This was her response to my complaint about a name that I thought was flat and nonresonant. I thought, my mother knew that about me; she had known more than I ever cared to believe.

Late that night when I was in bed, the phone rang and I decided not to pick up, knowing that it would be Michel. I placed a pillow over my head and waited for the rings to subside. It stopped and after ten minutes it started again. I regretted not having unplugged the phone the first time and picked up the receiver.

"Why didn't you pick up, Hélène? I was half dead with anguish that something had happened."

"I didn't hear," I heard myself say.

"Then put the damn phone next to the bed!"

I got out of bed and walked to the window with the phone in hand.

"I don't believe this. Who are you to talk to me like that? Honestly, who are you, Michel?"

There was a pause on either side of the receiver, and I went on.

"How can you do that? You're screaming at me! All the way from England! All the way from across the ocean! You're screaming at me because I made you think for five minutes that you had missed the day! Great comfort I should take in your little anguish. My husband's worried, oh my God! Why didn't I think of putting the phone next to the bed in case he decided to call in the middle of the night? How could I be so selfish as to instill the doubt in his mind that maybe—maybe our child was born?" I hung up and unplugged this time.

Of course I didn't sleep. I was enraged. A rage so physical that it turned my fists into knots and my nails into prongs.

I was ready for them: all of them. My anger needed room and I spaced out in it.

I pictured Michel and his self-centered angst for not being there where he should have been. I had pushed him to go. I had tested him and the result was limpid—clearer than my third home pregnancy test: Michel would always put his career first. At least I knew what to expect. Had I not known all along?

Then there was Thomas. Thomas and his clever ambivalence, his subtle flirting, his flammable youth under the white or black robe. Damn him if he thought his priesthood-to-be would protect him. He had put me on a burner, and I needed to bend him. I needed to see him crawl and beg.

In the end and by the first light of day, my body surrendered and I dozed off for a while.

Two hours later I got up and drew the curtains open. Thomas was there across the street on the sidewalk. He was smoking and looking around. He was moving his feet a lot; he seemed to be shooting little things into the gutter. He didn't wear a robe or a collarino. He had a raincoat on and had lifted the collar up as in a fifties movie. It crossed my mind that he had envisioned this look as more man-like, and I found it quite hysterical under the dazzling sun. He was taking long puffs and blowing the smoke upward. People on the street walked past him, and no one seemed to notice; some of them would just angle their way around him. All of this I could witness without being spotted; the glass of my bedroom window shoveled the morning light right back onto the street. My next move was to push the window wide open to let the air and the rest come in.

Thomas looked up at once. He started saying something and then thought better of it. He put out his Lucky under his shoe and started crossing. It must have been my facial expression alone that made him lean back and dodge the blue Mustang whooshing by like a bullet. Mustang. Bang. Thomas leaned back and I leaned forward onto the window ledge and lost my balance. I grabbed one of the sides and somehow made it back inside, but the move had made me squish my abdomen onto the windowsill. Something had been ruptured, and a sharp, shocking sting fired off inside.

For what must have been a few minutes, I lay on the floor like a beached mammal with a pain so intense I thought I was blind. The pain was a fierce and shapeless light I was forced to behold. In some remote part of the house, Thomas was banging on a door and calling my name. Then something was smashed open, and he was there next to me, kneeling.

"Down on your knees . . ." I uttered with a faint smile.

"Shush. Where's the phone?"

"Bedside . . ." I looked up in the right direction, and he picked up the receiver and started dialing.

"No tone! What's going on? For God's sake! What's going on?"

"Unplugged." Something was warm and spilling under me.

"Accident . . . Corner of Altadena and Casitas . . . We need an ambulance now. Now please! Okay." Thomas put the receiver down and knelt next to me again.

"They're coming, Hélène. Hang in there." He reached out for my forehead and pushed out a strand of hair, pulling it behind my ear. This was the most physical we had ever gotten to be.

"I wanted you . . . I wanted you to crawl."

"Don't talk. You don't have to talk. Just try to breathe slowly, okay?"

"Okay." I closed my eyes for a while, and I tried to think of Thomas's hand and how warm it was. I couldn't stop wanting it. The pain wouldn't defeat the want. The pain attracted the want like a magnet. I could not rid myself of it. I tried not to think about the warm fluid under me and the warm child inside me. I cried a bit.

∽

In the emergency room, they didn't ask a lot of questions. Thomas was allowed in there as if it was all-natural, as if our bond spoke for itself. They let him fill in the paperwork under my muted directions. Thomas was there until they pushed me on a gurney into an operating room with bright overhead lights. I saw him wave as they closed the green double doors on him. The woman doctor spoke like a machine gun. She said I had a placental abruption and they needed to get my child out fast. They put me to sleep.

❦

When I emerged, Thomas was on a stool next to my bed. He spoke first.

"He made it."

"A boy?"

"A baby boy."

I wiped my face with both hands, stretching the skin to the side, holding it there—the Japanese look.

"I should go now. I'll tell them you're awake."

"Will you come and visit?"

"No."

"Why not?"

"Because I'm not meant to . . . because . . . that's it."

"That's it?" I lifted myself onto my elbows.

Thomas stood from the stool and almost made it fall just like he had on our first meet. He started for the door. He moved in slow motion, his shoes squeaking on the linoleum floor.

"I don't know if I can do this," I said as he reached the door. And I knew I was lying as I spoke the words. I knew I would be fine: a mother and a wife; a good life. Everything but a great lover. And then, resisting with all my will an impulse to scream and call him back, I swallowed hard.

Rêve

Y ou will ask me about the word humanity with the
TV remote in your hand. You will sit in your jam-
mies on the brown sofa, and the TV will be blasting
music: the sort of discombobulated music that works as a
Google translator for emotions. Music will say "be scared"
and you will be a little scared. You will want to be scared
because the music will say so. And when the music stops,
you will repeat your question about humanity . . . you will
smile with the overlapping incisors, and I will notice the
dimple on your left cheek. I will not understand how you
can be so little and so black and so smiley in the middle of
your question.

I will have a hard time focusing because of the TV. I, too,
will want to follow the orders dispensed by the music, but I
will also want to answer your question in a way that makes
sense. I will not like my confusion. I will criticize myself
for that. I will be aware that TV-induced mix-up does not
necessarily work as a good excuse for not answering your
question. Still, I will be grateful for the TV to hide my per-
plexity. I will be consoled by the characters in the TV do-

ing what they are expected to do. I will buy time by asking you if you want a sip of water. You will say yes and ask for me to add something in the water to make it more flavorful. A stick of melon? I will ask.

You lived for three years in a place where water only comes in yellow "improved buckets" with a constraining lid to dissuade hand entry; the result being a damaged intestine and an everlasting taste for flavored water. I will never have seen the place where water only comes in buckets, but I will have read about it and I will imagine it, and my imagination will have its own memory. I will have forgotten nothing of the place that crafted your small and fragile intestine.

This is the day you follow me to the kitchen to watch me cut the melon open—bright orange and glistening on the inside like a fresh, flapping head. You will like the kitchen better than the TV because of all the food, because of all the mystery of the food, a mystery much greater than the mystery of the TV. I will not be able to deny enjoying the fact that you are looking at me in wonder, as if I am the Great Priestess about to accomplish the divine sacrifice. I will be rather nauseated, like always when I touch a knife and a fruit. You will ask if you can do it, please, and I will see no reason not to, even though something visceral inside me will scream to not let you, because in my mind's eye you will cut yourself, and an ocean of blood will gush out of you, and your warm blackness will turn gray, and I will curl my body around yours on the floor, but even so I will not be able to make you warm, and you will not be able to make me warm either.

And when that does not happen, when you will just cut the piece of melon and stick it in the pitcher with three ice cubes, they will have the sound a child makes. You will pick two glasses with blue decals of sea turtles in a cupboard that will be a little too high for you, and you will have to grab a stool and go on your toes. This will be way before you are tall and robust with an afro.

You will have no trouble pouring the water from the pitcher and letting go of the ice cubes on the edge, *bling*— and then you will click your tongue in anticipation—*tlick*. But still you will give me my glass first, and you will wait for me to drink before you start.

I will thank you with no more than one word.

While I drink, I will have the answer to your question, but I will not know how to put it into words without letting go of the ice cubes in my mouth.

⌒ Ten years old ⌒

You will not ask me anything. You will just show up in the doorframe in your white boxer shorts while we are having dinner with the ambassador and his wife. There will be no drums before you come in. There will just be you in the doorframe, and you will look taller and blacker than usual because of the subdued lighting and the contrast with your boxer shorts.

It will take a minute before I will realize you are here. It will take the ambassador asking. I will not know what to do. I will be stunned by my incapacity to improvise. I will be glued to my chair, and I will want to know what to do. I will want quick wit and humor. I will make a wish to stand and walk toward the doorframe and take you by the arm and make you sit at the table with the ambassador and his wife.

Your eyes will wander in the vague.

You lived for three years on the verge of starvation, the result being a small ledge of your ribs above the stomach and stray eyes when hunger visits you. I will never have starved. I was brought up with the notion that I should always leave the table feeling a bit hungry. I will not have met hunger, but I will meet the wander in your eyes. I will ask God if he knew what he was doing when he gave you to me and me to you.

The ambassador will nod.

You will step out of the doorframe and head back to your room. You will be swallowed by the darkness of the hallway. I will try to discern you from the darkness as you walk backward, but my eyes will not be able to adjust. I will close my eyes in the hope of beating the light. I will re-member the night I tried to take a picture of you and your friends, and my phone would not detect you.

In my mind's eye you will not be there. You will never come back; the hallway will consume you. I will run to your bedroom, and your bed will vanish below the carpet, and your smell will float out of reach behind the wall surface. I will destroy the wall with an axe, and your smell will move to the basement. I will rush to the basement and remember that there is no basement in our house, and your smell will shift below ground and I will bury myself, but even so I will not find you, and you will not find me again, ever.

And when that does not happen, when I just excuse myself for a minute, you will sit on your bed and pat the space next to you; that will make me want to cry. You will say that you woke up and you heard us and it sounded fun and it smelled good. I will ask if you want to eat something, and you will say that you took some bread from the kitchen. I will kiss you on your cheek, and you will have the taste of bread and salt crystals. This will be way before you shave.

You will have no trouble imagining your future, and this is the day you tell me you will become a chef, and you lift your eyebrows out of joy at your discovery.

I will not know what to say. There will be nothing to say.

I will let you sleep with breadcrumbs on your bedsheets, and I will return to the ambassador and his wife.

〜 Thirty years old 〜

I will stand in the middle of your restaurant. You will ask me to come. I will stand there and notice your tall and white chef's hat behind the framed counter. There will be nothing that prepares me for that. There will be you and the tall and white chef's hat that takes hold of you, and there will be the shock of that.

It will take a minute before you realize I am here. It will take a blonde waitress turning her head a little in my direction. You will break into a smile, and I will stand here, magnetized, on the waxed concrete floor. I will smile back a bit stupidly, and you will squeeze me with a kiss and a hug from behind the counter. The blonde and braided waitress will carry me away to a peaceful corner and glide a cushioned chair under me. I will come across the distraction of your decorum. There will be two chandeliers and no candle lights. I will be taken by surprise by the relief I feel from the presence of one and the absence of the other.

Your restaurant will be quiet. There will be acoustic foam tiles on your ceiling. There will be acoustic foam tiles on some of the walls. All that soundproofing will soothe me like the padded silence between us. I will wonder whether that habit of the hushed quiet comes from me. I will love to think about that while I will observe you from my table. I will see you talking to your employees. There will be the voluble you and the mute me. There will be the authoritative you and the hesitant me. I will wonder what I would say to you if I was more talkative. I will wonder whether my lack of words is a presence to you and whether that is why, every time I am speechless, you make space for me with your own words. Still, I will regret my limitations. I will regret not standing next to you in the kitchen and talking through the rest of the evening and the rest of the night. And the next morning. I will regret not placing a hand on your shoulder to feel your warmth and make you feel mine. . Vapor will float up from the soup on the next table.

The blonde waitress will come and recite the specials like

a fable. There will be a dish named after me, and I will lose her after that. I will feel giddy. I will look for you but you will have left your post, and you will no longer be visible from where I sit. The waitress will be waiting for my order. I will hold my breath in the hope of hearing your voice beyond the muffled atmosphere of the dining tables. I will hear nothing, only white noise like radio static. In my mind's eye you will pass out in the kitchen, and they will try to revive you. I will see one of your employees shouting for help, but I will not hear him. I will be mute and I will be deaf. I will sit inside my body, and you will lie in yours. When the paramedics will take you on the gurney, I will scream a scream too fragile to travel outside of me. You will never hear me again, and I will never hear you again.

And when that does not happen, I will order only two appetizers. The restaurant will empty out as I take small bites. You will emerge from your kitchen with your hat still planted on top of your head. You will carry a tiny, dark dessert topped with a white lump that looks a lot like an egg. You will allow yourself to sit with me, and you will purse your lips and sigh a contented sigh. This will be way before your babies kick inside the blonde waitress's womb.

Then you will ask me what I thought, and I will place my hand in front of me to signal that I cannot talk with my mouth full.

〜 Ninety-five years old 〜

I will have a question for you—when will you visit next?

I will pick up the phone and dial your number. I will be lying in bed with an old-fashioned receiver in my hand. It will be the sort of phone that does not exist anywhere but in geriatric departments. I will think that someone has decided that old phones are appropriate for old people. The windows will be inoperable. Like me. Everything will match me. And the other old woman with whom I will share this room.

While the phone rings, I will turn my question over in my head many times. I will rehearse it. I will catch you in your apartment looking for that phone that keeps ringing. I will measure how long it will take you to get to the phone. Your phone will be misplaced, and time will stretch between now and the moment I ask what I have to ask. I will pinch the cartilage of my ear with the plastic of the receiver. I will massage the tilt of my hip with my other hand.

There will be the interruption of the old woman. She will shout to be taken home. She will be hard to ignore. I will appease her out of generosity and because I want to be able to have a last phone conversation with you without her interrupting all the time. I will tell her that her daughter will come and pick her up tomorrow like she said she would. She will ask me if I am sure and I will be sure. She will fall back asleep and die sometime before morning.

The phone will keep ringing. I will pull up the collar of the gown that I have been wearing for days. Cold air-snakes will wiggle over the bedsheets and under where there will be holes. I will look at your picture beside my bed and check the temperature of the grain of your skin. I will feel the weight of the coat of my skin. I will weigh how much we are the constant photographs of our respective foreignitude. I will know that you would hold me tight if you knew I had such visions.

You will not pick up the phone. Not because it was misplaced but because something will have happened to you. I will be unable to see with my mind's eye. I will not know what has happened to you, which will be much worse than when I am picturing things. It will be worse than the worst because it will be unimaginable. I will put the receiver back on its base, and I will rub my eyes and the cartilage of my ear with the unimaginable.

And when that does not happen, when the old-fashioned phone rings, it will be you calling me back. You will ask me how I am doing, and you will add Mama at the end of your question in the way you always say it. I will not need to ask you when you will visit next. Because there will be nothing to ask.

You will let me doze with your voice in my ear.

MRI

Thirty minutes into the procedure, Mathias Drane, a bike courier, tightens his neck muscles to lift his head from the scanner table, noticing again that his forehead is held in straps, as are his hands, as is his chest. Although thirty minutes is a conjecture, it seems to him a fair assessment, in line with the tingling feeling in his right calf; he rotates his ankle and bends his toes. The tingling doesn't go away. With more ankle-rotation, the tingling eventually goes. It is the first time he has an MRI—the first time his body slips entirely into a tube. In some way, it is an experience, something fresh, like the first time he saw Juliane, like his first downhill time-trial race, like crashing his bike into a cliff. At noon, a compassionate doctor declared his body officially broken, and now he is waiting for the final decree, which will come out of the box where he now lies.

There is a miniscule drop of water condensed on the surface of the tube right in front of him. He looks at the drop; he blinks a lot—he always blinks a lot—feeling the stillness of the air around him. The only atmospheric motion in the tube comes from his own breathing. He exhales through his nostrils and feels the small gust traveling over his philtrum and further out. He follows the breath-volute around in the tube—up it goes, and then down again. He feels like an opium smoker in his own cloud, smoking his own breath. He floats needlessly. There is pleasure in that sensation. The condensed drop is about to roll. He has no idea how he knows that: that the liquid pearl will set itself in motion, that gravity will pull on the delicate skin of the pearl and distort its shape. He knows. While the drop knows nothing about itself, about the vapor that made it, and yet in a second it will drop onto his face—shameless. He makes elaborate computations about the probable point of contact. His nose bridge—the drop will navigate onto his nose bridge, not for very long, then flow through to his cheek, down his jawline, along the upper part of his neck, and will end on the surface of the scanner with a plip. It's as if, lying there in this tube, he's both the weatherman and the weather map.

There is a loud rushing noise, like a whipping noise with a small bird at the end of it. Mathias is wearing earplugs, but he can hear it very clearly. It is not so much the loudness as it is the repetitiveness that is striking. Every thirty seconds or so, there is a loud alarm sound like a foghorn, followed by more horns and then claps as if someone wearing oversized clogs was walking and tripping around the tube. In an effort to deflect the noise, Mathias closes his eyes and imagines himself at the top of a very steep hill on his bike. He can throw himself full speed down the hill

184 ● A Gypsy's Book of Revelation

with as much realism as one sitting with goggles in a 3D theater. He experiences such ease and looseness in his trip that he suspects at once that he could be falling asleep— the effect of the Diazepam. If that's the case, he will resist. He doesn't want unconsciousness. Not now.

He jumps to thinking that there is no such thing as chance, that everything is linked, Juliane would say. It is no accident that precisely this morning before the crash, he received her package in his mailbox, a stack of photos. She could have sent an email with the pictures as attachments, a link to a Dropbox if the files were too big. Instead she picked a brown paper envelope, licked a series of antique stamps, went to the post office in Boseong, which, according to a short consultation of the Internet, is located on the southern shore of South Korea. His mind wanders back to the inscription on the sticky note affixed on top of the stack. *For you, my dearest Mathias, with all my love.* Nothing else. He closes his eyes and visualizes the inscription again, the elegant tilt of the letters. His mind stays there for a while; it drifts like a bird on her aquatic words. He swallows his saliva—warm and salty. He presses his head deeper in the pillow that the operator added for his comfort.

Gazing upward at the strips of fluorescent light on either side of him, at the white plastic surface of the tube, Mathias doesn't see plastic. Mathias sees Juliane's skin, pale and microscopically textured. There is a bit of sweat behind her knees and at the base of the neck, and there is one drop entirely formed between her shoulder blades—about to roll.

There is one mosquito trying to get through the bed canopy, called in by the blood pulsing in the wrists of the sleeper. Hzzzz. Nothing for a while. Hzzzzz. It is sixteen hours later in Korea; the sun is rising there. Outside Juliane's bungalow, the clouds are kissing the cliffs. Vapor comes off the ground. Someone is burning incense nearby. It smells of a warm and powdery and almost creamy wood.

Mathias tries to shift position, but of course he can't. His sense of smell—always acute—seems to have sharpened. He smells the odor of the MRI operator. It is an honest smell—overlaid with the bleachy and soupy hospital smell but unmistakably human and a little citrusy. It travels toward him and into the tube like a meteorite, and with it comes something smoky as well—the morning spell of Juliane in Boseong. And now he wonders about this elation of his, this capacity to recreate Juliane in all her fundamentals: her skin, her smell, her sweat. Perhaps it is how she wants to manifest herself in him: like a fearless explorer, a pioneer of her own body, a freedom fighter able to break the distance with a few photos. When he, Mathias, really never travels any farther than a few hundred miles away from home—with his padded pants, his cycling glasses, and a breathable rain jacket *just in case*. It is a bit depressing to think that he hasn't changed, that all his riding hasn't made him more of a man, that his tan is all but on the surface, that his apparent health is just for display. He still feels like himself: a sickly, shy boy silent in a group of adults who ask him questions that he never answers. Because he can't. Because he doesn't know what to say.

There is a voice—out of nowhere—feminine and calm. "How are you, Mr. Drane?" the voice asks. He focuses simplemindedly on the meaning of the question. There is more than one truthful answer. He is working his mental way through the tangle of the words to be honest. "Mr. Drane, are you okay?" the voice asks, now with a slightly more pronounced upward intonation. He is about to respond. At the same time, he is very much conscious of the futility of this dialogue. In a way, he doesn't wish to answer. So he doesn't. "Mr. Drane, we have another thirty minutes to go. I need to know that you're okay or we'll have to get you out and start all over again. Can you hear me at least?"

"Yes." He thrusts the word out with superhuman effort, pushing either side of his tongue against his upper premolars, pulling his lips out into his cheeks. On a three-second time scale, it starts out with the wetness of the "*iii*," rolls forward to the "*eee*," glides into the "*sss*," which skids ahead until it pulls his mouth shut. Once it is said, he feels the impact of a thought in the lower left part of his brain—like a rubber arrow. He feels like a nine-month-old saying "yes" for the first time.

"Thank you," the voice says, audibly irritated.

Bing. The tremor is gone. That is all. What is left is a mild yet lingering sense of being exposed.

And then he holds on for what, two minutes without hardly thinking?

The side light in the tube flickers. It's a slight flicker, perhaps more like a very brief dimming that corresponds to another machine turning on. The MRI operator has most likely noticed it. He should wait it out and see whether it happens again. If it happens again, he doesn't want to miss it. And so he tries not to blink for a while, which is hard. His eyes water, and a tear swells and escapes to the exterior edge on the right side. Now he is crying. It hurts and it soothes—it does both. He lets himself go. The tears come, not as a sprinkle, not as a downpour, but as a deluge. Part of him is precipitated onto the scanner. In a moment, the scanner temperature will make his teardrops evaporate and perhaps reform above him. Suddenly he has this flashing memory of a school book in seventh grade: a naïve blue sea and a bright yellow sun, a white cloud, oversized blue raindrops, a meandering river on a green mountain. *C'est comme ça qu'on fait la pluie.* He liked French in school. *Il ne faut pas pleurer, Mathias, ça ne sert vraiment à rien.*

Being in this tube may provoke tachycardia, the doctor said. The doctor shouldn't have said that. Saying things makes them happen. Saying I love you in a drunk delirium made him love Juliane—it wasn't the other way around. And words are irreversible. Mathias cannot unsay I love you; the doctor cannot walk back on his warning. So there is flopping in his chest. Mathias's heart beats too fast; he breathes too often.

"Everything okay, Mr. Drane?"

Juliane is here again. She has this irritating way of re-

turning. She is very much like this upsetting refrain, which
Mathias hums quietly in the tube—about absence, about
how it's there—a hole in the middle of everything—about
how it's always the same hole.

He should stop humming, he should stop summoning
Juliane. But that's not him—he can't stop. And all the
while as he hums, he sees himself when he was little
(eight?). Eight-year-old Mathias makes a bet. The bet
is to cross a square lined with chestnut trees filled with
starlings. It is raining shit on the square—intensely. He
needs to run through and dodge it. That is his way to
confront shit—head-on. He almost makes it. He gets hit
in the very last yard, right when he is opening his mouth
to cry victory. This is when he stops humming and starts
laughing inwardly. Juliane says he scoffs at everything
valuable about himself—including his resolve. Still, it's
funny, she must admit it. The voice calls out to him again,
reiterates her question.

This time, his "yes" is effortless, sincere.

The light flickers again. He's thirsty.

He feels like having one of those sports drinks—with
added minerals and electrolytes—something really re-
freshing, with cucumber mint flavor. He has a collection
at home—little tabs that dissolve into his plastic water
bottles. The collection sits in the pantry on the uppermost
shelf, just above the assortment of energy bars. Juliane says
that Mathias's pantry looks like a medicine cabinet. She
says a real pantry smells of apples in a crate, of sawdust and

permanent humidity, which is another way of saying that a real pantry is a morgue for food with preferably northern orientation and no windows. And him, with his tubes and bars, he is trying to escape the pantry rule. He likes food so unfoodlike, so abstract that the idea of death cannot touch it. Nothing can rot in there. Not even the pickled vegetables on the lower shelf. In fact, he's trying to turn his pantry on its head, to make it a chamber of eternal, color-ful life-pellets and ever-enduring fermented food, a place he can crawl into when the world explodes. He does what he can with what he has.

A side ache starts to run on the left side of his head. Mathias did not think a side ache could reside in the head. He assumed like everyone else that a side ache dwells un-der the rib cage. But now he's feeling this stabbing pain that compares accurately to a side ache. It starts with a sharp swelling sensation, like rising sea waters. And once attain-ing its maximum intensity, the pain sloshes back and forth, as if stuck in his long and narrow skull. Mathias doesn't seem to be equipped with the necessary mental sluiceways. In short, he is going through a cerebral climate change, an expression that would no doubt delight Juliane.

There is the sound of clogs moving in the adjacent room not far. The room has a screen that displays all his bodily commotion. In a way, it must be entertaining, like some special exhibition—Mathias's Side Ache or The Rising Blur. But if it comes to a choice between allowing his bro-ken body to be on display and pedaling in the sauerkraut,

Mathias would rather ride in his own cabbage. The side ache must be beautiful by now: Blazing Sun in Skull.

"Mr. Drane. How do you feel?"

"Fine."

"Any pain?"

"Mmmmm."

"Where?"

"The head."

"On a scale from one to ten, how would you rate the pain?"

Mathias calls on the worst possible pain he can imagine. Like being skinned alive with a peeling knife, bit by bit, starting with his extremities—a ten. On that scale, the scale that ends with the skinning, the side ache rates a solid four.

"Four."

"We'll go on then. Would you like me to turn on the radio gently so you can listen to music through the rest of the procedure?"

". . . No."

He just said *no* exactly like Juliane—like a short and disconnected note—after a small rest—followed by the noticeable absence of *thank you*. And because he said *no* just like her, Mathias knows that the ache in his side will not leave him anymore. It is here to stay. The pain has progressed to a new stage; it is becoming part of the whole that defines him. Mathias has clear blue eyes, a yellow road bike, and a side ache on the left side of his head. When he emerges from the tube, his head will be slightly tilted to the left, as if someone had driven a screw to his skull, wound a yarn around it, and tied a calibration weight at the end. The weight will change under the dedicated effort of an invisible hand—it should not remain the same at all times because it is constantly adjusted, and that makes it alive. Mathias can accept alive pain. The only thing that Mathias is truly afraid of is to feel nothing, something until now he could combat with a 2:00 a.m. bike ride on the hills near the ravines.

Did the operator put on the radio even though he said not to? No. He just imagines it, but the idea of music gets on his nerves, and layers an oddly familiar form of violence with his pain. Mathias starts having terrible thoughts. Thoughts that get stuck in his heart like rust spots on his bike chain. He's in a tube that has dissolved all sense of outsideness. He is so enclosed in himself that the violence budding in him feels as unprompted and irrepressible as an epileptic seizure. He's thankful to be fully strapped, and at the same time, his leg muscles tighten as if they may rupture. Tendons and hollows get drawn around his muscles—barely covered in skin. He feels unnerved and tight, about to burst at the seams, fully disqualified to exist outside of this tube. Right now, he could hurt Juliane, pull one of her eyes out of its socket, burn the skin on her breasts with a lighter, kiss her in a way that would choke her—catching the nose and the mouth all at once—and wait. It's a feeling of evil joy and immense distress, a feeling close to what Juliane once described to him as the philosophy of a poet whose name he forgot, but whose words wedged into his cortex:

"The unique and supreme delight lies in the certainty of doing 'evil'—and men and women know from birth that all pleasure lies in evil.

"But what can eternity of damnation matter to someone who has felt, if only for a second, the infinity of delight?"

And as usual his violence spurt comes in spasms and is already receding. It's a little like sex or like jet lag, in that it is the accumulation of little waves—of pleasure, of fatigue—that gradually build up to a seaquake, which crashes to the ground and then shatters into pieces. It is delightful and shameful and exhausting. Once it is over, it is over. If he hadn't become a bike courier, he wouldn't have quit smoking, and it would be time for a cigarette or a joint, like after the battle, like after the rain, like after the procedure. Juliane once told him about a trip she took to Jordan—before they met—where she was invited to a private room in a restaurant, and they passed around an *argileh* full of marinated tobacco and molasses. As she told him the story of the pipe being passed around, he could visualize the smoke getting out of her lips—coming out like a dream, rolling out—every last bit. It makes him happy to relive that story she told him. He smiles with his lips closed. He says to himself that it was the right move to tie him in this tube, where he is protected by the warmth of his imagination. He doesn't care that he is wrecked, that perhaps he's going to die, that the machine will confirm his sentence. He may as well smoke his last pipe here, eat his last supper, watch the sunset, hold Juliane's hand, choke her with a kiss, pedal away. He can do all of this here, and the machine will not stop him. The machine will settle for projecting splashes of color onto the operator's screen, and it will look nice and incomprehensible.

Observing his own thought is dry and infinite like the desert—a clean process with a lot of recycling involved. There is a recurrent meandering to it, which snakes a bit like a Brazilian dance. Mathias is a good dancer—all types of dances. It's one thing he can claim without second-guessing himself. When he was an adolescent, his friends admired him for a particular series of dancing steps he could execute at full speed onto any rhythm. He can still do it, although he has less opportunity as he gets older. Not long ago he attended a workshop close to his apartment—mostly cha-cha-cha. He tried to teach Juliane one night, and he owes to that the only moment he ever held her tight.

Mathias's lower left leg lifts up and hits the tube before it goes back down—the first of six steps. It strikes him how the memory of dancing is all in his muscles, his nerves, in the privacy of his connective tissues. It soothes him to think about dancing because it is done without thinking—or if it is thinking, it is a very ancient form of it, a form that seeps into his bone marrow. Once dancing is learned, it cannot be forgotten, like biking. The body knows forever. Only in death will they part: his body and the dancing. And even then, how would he know what will be happening inside his dead matter? If nails continue to grow for a while, the same inertia must leave the memory of dancing somewhere.

Perhaps the tube is growing on him. It is a bit like a house growing on an older person. There is this moment where having been in one place for so long, a node gets formed between the content and the container. This is where the light flickered and the eyes winked. This is where his opioid breath has curled and met with the white plastic surface before it fell back down and he could smoke his own odor as if it was pure Afghan. This is where his heels define the end of the tube and where the tube defines the end of him. This is where the strap inlays his forehead. This is where his skin has sealed with the tube, and no one can tell whether it can be unglued. He's tired now; he starts fossilizing.

Somewhere something makes the sound of a buzzer and there is motion. Whether the motion is Mathias's or the tube's is impossible to sort out. It is as if Mathias has been sitting on a train for a long time and the landscape starts to move—the first impression is that the land is moving, not the train. The sun rises at the end of the tube, the floor beneath him drops as if in an elevator, yet Mathias is still lying on the firm, glassy surface. There is this idea, a bit panicky, that he is an astronomer stepping out of his shuttle into infinity. It's so bright out there, so painful to the eyes. He closes them tight. In that short moment, he fears that some essential piece of equipment will fail—his hair will get caught, he will get partly scalped, the straps that tie him to the tube will rupture and he will impale himself onto something sharp, he will lose control and urinate and set off multiple short-circuits, leading to abundant electrical contact burns—the smell of his carbonized flesh will make the operator pass out and there will be no help. Obviously, beneath this shell of stress, Mathias is excited; the hair on his arms spikes up like a platoon of miniature toy soldiers. As he glides out of the tube, he stretches in length, he fills his lungs with a big breath, he feels what all creatures feel as they step into a new world—an urge to shout out and expel the overflow of euphoria, the spirit of conquest. Mathias gliding out of the tube is Tarzan swinging out of the forest. And now he opens his eyes wide and lifts his eyebrows to help. He decides he likes it here—the muted pale green color, the cleanliness of the ceiling tiles, the rows of neon lights that seem to guide out to an invisible yet heavenly exit.

"We're done," the operator says.

She's pretty—not as pretty as Juliane but pretty. With slightly darker skin around her eyes, the near absence of eyebrows, her round face, her fine hair tied in a ponytail, and a somewhat frozen smile, she has a dignified yet enigmatic look. A medical Sphynx—minus the cruelty. She has the look of someone launching into interior debate about how she will say what she will say next.

Part of Mathias would like to help her: the romantic part. That part would like to talk and say that he knows already and that there is no need to take oratory precautions. It's a chivalrous instinct—generous and self-guided. In the millisecond that follows, Mathias feels valiant, able to brave the danger. When unstrapped from the machine, he will rise and stand tall, hold the operator in his arms, embrace her impetuously, tell her it is okay, not to talk, not to worry. They will elope and seize the days that are left, taking sunny breakfasts under the olive trees. But if Mathias looks closer, deeper into his desires, if he allows the clarity of mind that accompanies the certainty of his death, where he truly sees himself, where he truly wants himself, is in an extraordinary freefall—out of a small airplane, a very loud machine, a propeller-driven aircraft. There, knees bent over the edge, the door wide open, the wind frantically beating his hair onto his face, he will watch the curvature of the earth, and before that at the forefront, a small and shy cloud, full of melancholic dampness. He will hold on to the fuselage, his knuckles temporarily white under the gloves, his body will make one with the plane, and he will let go, tumble into the air as in a drum-type washing machine, no up and no down, the blue and the brown dancing like the remnants of lights from a disco ball, followed by the calm: his body flattened into a napkin, his legs and arms bent out of the way. That is all.

"Would you like a glass of water?" the Sphynx asks as she touches the skin on his forehead with her very cold hands while untying the straps.

"Please."

He must sit before he stands. Quietly, he tightens the muscles in his abdominals. It is a gigantic effort, mobilizing all his strength; he feels like an old self summoned out of a deep chair. The room has no windows, and it is cold in here. There is a clock tied perpendicularly to the wall to his left, a round white analog clock. Time flows normally and the operator walks across the room toward a small metal sink. He is starting to rise out of his lying position and feels some light-headedness as gravity plays tricks with his blood flow. He helps himself with his hands pressed onto the sides of the scanner-bed. The hospital gown slips from his shoulders as he sits. Facing away from him, the operator fills a paper cup at the sink. He closes his eyes. This time there'll be no trouble hearing what she won't say; there is nothing that can stop that now. His body damage is no longer a concept. The machine has captured it and marked him like cattle. He is branded for the same reason livestock has been since ancient times, to prove ownership. The damage owns him. He fits himself on the scanner, adjusts the gown back up, expels a small excess of air. The Sphynx comes back to him with the paper cup held forward. He takes it gently from her hand. There's always this, he thinks, and the photos. And he drinks slowly, letting water drown the last of his resistance. And finally, progressively as if on a dimmer, the hope to see Juliane again is turned off.

Home

"No, it is home to me. I'm headed home."

The man in the seat next to me looked startled, as if I had answered that I was born two million years ago. He was wearing an outfit with several shades of blue. He pulled back as much as the airplane seat would allow and resting both hands on the armrest between us, his face still, he stared at me as if looking for bits of this odd place I was calling home. That I sat on a plane headed to the improbable country of my childhood seemed to me as extraordinary as the fact that it could be someone's homeland to this man. I looked away and started thinking about my mother, who was the motive for this trip. She was the only remnant of my entire family. Over my years of absence, they had all died, one by one, young and old, like the last wilted curls surrounding a bald spot. No one had waited. An image of my mother started to form and with it the spatial discomfort that I always felt in her presence. I could never create space between me and my mother, certainly not on a plane. She had vacuum cleaned at dawn and banged into my bedroom door. She had ironed my clothes in the entryway in her underwear. She had never kissed me good night however; out of modesty, I assumed. I had left my homeland and not seen her for two decades. I had woken up in the middle of one night, tried writing, and within days I had booked a ticket.

Through the slot of the window, the mountains moved toward us, like enormous chocolate breasts; their curves licked by heavy taupe vapors. Farther out, the horizon bent into sepia smudges that looked primitive. This vision was enough to rule out hope that the liveliness I remembered was still there. The bed of thinning rivers spilled like white ink on blotting paper. An entire forest was down, trees uprooted, laid to rest with their branches extended behind them, like splayed dogs looking for freshness. I forced myself to keep watching.

My neighbor was back in his original position, his knees hooked on the backrest of the seat ahead, his temple pushed against the folded wing of the headrest. He had stopped staring at me; neither the brown mountains nor the fallen forest seemed to interest him.

I leaned against the wall behind the window and used my bag as a pillow. I had no illusion that I could sleep; my right hand shook when I tried to hold it flat. My eyes were shot with fatigue and yet I could follow the terrain like a nighttime passenger follows the roadsides lit up by the headlights. This mountain chain led to the desert and to the valley and to the city by the ocean and then out to my village. From within my eyelids if I closed my eyes, I could extend the road to the post office and on to the small boulevard after the traffic light and to the right over the trail and into the cul-de-sac up the hill where my house stood on the last fork. This mental path was as well lit as a landing strip. I asked a stewardess where we were and how long we had until landing: she said about two hours.

I must have been about to nod off when I felt a violent jolt. The air inside the plane looked inflamed, as if the particles of dust had been lit up by the setting sun. The clouds outside were gathering and covering the view below; I could almost smell their humidity. Somewhere in the back of the plane, a baby started crying. I rolled my earplugs into small thin snakes that slid agreeably into my ear canals. I closed my eyes.

A lamp lit up beside me. Perhaps my neighbor wanted to read. Yet he hadn't struck me as the reading type. I opened one eye to check and I thought I recognized the pattern of the fabric on the seat in front of me. It wasn't a woven fabric but rather a plush velvet material in a forest green shade. I couldn't place where I had seen that fabric, and this lapse saddled me with a tip of the tongue stubbornness. One of the earplugs fell. I opened the other eye. The lights were now very bright, creating a glare that prevented me from distinguishing much yet. I could just smell the odor of the air around and feel a draft on my cheek, something fresh and vivid and humid like when someone just opened a window. My curiosity was wide awake. I rubbed my eyes and sat up to see better. Someone shouted, "Yeti!"

No one since middle school had called me by this name. I had learned to respond to many names during my existence overseas. Good or bad names that strangers had created to compensate awkward and sometimes delightful pronunciations. Names that had been given to me in booths of cafés, in meeting rooms, in stores, in lavatories, on the phone, on immigration documents, on letterheads, on delivery packages, on mailboxes. During my nights of insomnia, when I had been counting the breaths of my husband, I had hoped to hear him murmur this old name in his sleep; but it had been lost, this name that tricked me to think that it could make me "me" again, that it could make me sleep at last and start fresh the next morning, with my people, a life that was irrecoverable. As my old name rang in my ears, I pulled my thumb toward my mouth to eat the skin around my nail, even though this gesture had earned me much admonishing as a child. I was surprised to see that a full layer of skin had disappeared, leaving my thumb to look like a peeled beet, my nail so short it barely covered half of the phalange.

The seat ahead of me now seemed enveloped in the excess of light that mashed into an emulsion, and there was a little mound of chestnut hair protruding from the backrest. Soon, a few strands of that hair set about flying off in my direction carried by the wind coming from the front of the cabin; I felt loose, unstiffened by the warmth of the stripes of yellow sun whizzing by my window.

The ruffled chestnut hair swirled around, and the face of my sister materialized on top of the headrest. With her pointed chin perched there, sixteen-year-old Jacqui looked at me sharply through the disc of her brown-rimmed glasses. The punch of her gaze hit me right above the stomach. I tried to control my breathing as in an effort to suppress a colossal hiccup. Once over the shock, a relief spread and hardened in me like egg white in a frying pan. Jacqui's face was fresh and her skin looked blonde and fuzzy as an apricot in the noon sun; her cheeks bore no sign of aging. I suddenly remembered that she inherited the glasses from our cousin Max, who had been a repeat runaway. Jacqui had adored Max, and while she had no vision problems to speak of, she had seized the glasses he had left behind and kept them on her nose. Memory, thrown to my face like a paintball, left me mute and puzzled yet with a wild mental energy that would not spread to my body. As she watched me, she looked resolute and curious and playful, her eyes round as if invisible matches were placed there to keep them wide open. She had two small lines at the top of her forehead, like flattened question marks. I had seen those lines many times during heated discussions at dinner, or when she was burying herself in homework, or when Lucian had asked her for a dance during the bonfires of autumn, also later during the marches against the orange government. The last time I had seen her round, goggled eyes and the thin, flat lines at the top of her forehead had been the day before I had left for good, in the bar-restaurant of our village where I had met her for coffee. I was surprised to have been able to forget her face, crowned by that unruly chestnut hair, whipping the confined air of the plane.

Above the seat next to Jacqui, the head of my brother Guil surfaced like a puppet. Guil and the depth of his blue eyes, his usual wit spread across his face. His good-looking adolescent gaze made me weak in the knees again. I had no doubt Guil knew the effect he had on me. Because he could always sense his own effect on others, like a slender dog, able to discern the smallest, most invisible change; such as the pace at which the veins under the skin contract or dilate under the rush of blood. I gave in to the joy of seeing him again; I gave in to the delicious fear of him. His hair, worn in a raised quiff style, was coarse and choppy as it flew up in the breezy atmosphere of the cabin—oddly balanced—like the bulrushes at the edge of the creek, as if small invisible pollen orbs dangled at the end of each strand, making them always swing back to their original place. A friend of the family had once said that Guil was a bit alien, which also meant that he had been lonely. His only defense had been a sense of irony that he had worn like a second skin. His other defense had been Jacqui.

Looking at them both propped on the seats ahead of me, my body was raided by a pleasing limpness. I felt helpless in a happy way, like I had been when they were shooting rapid-fire questions at me at the end of a long school day. There was something delectable in being with my older siblings again, carried up in the yellow evening air, feeling infinitely tired.

They smiled, looked at each other, and raised their eyebrows at the same time. And then as in a scene rehearsed many times, Guil took his arms off his tracksuit sleeves, and Jacqui disappeared behind him; her arms then materialized into his sleeves. Jacqui's hands started floating around Guil's head, scratching his ears, flattening his hair on his head, placing a fist in front of his lips mimicking a brushing gesture. Guil opened his mouth and showed off his straight teeth. Jacqui's hand picked up a fictional piece of salad and threw it at me. As a steward walked by with a drink tray, they both disappeared back into their seat.

I felt sad and upset. I was under the impression, like I used to be when I was at home with them, that I was excluded from their games and the warmth of their bond. They had died together, in a nighttime accident, with the music still playing in the car after the fact. I had wanted to ask them what they were talking about as it happened, if they were talking at all, or if they were just quietly together like they always had been.

I needed to go to the bathroom. I consciously registered that the plane had a two-four-two seating layout and that I sat in seat number 33A. It reassured me to reflect in this numbered way: it told me that, despite the momentary appearance of my dead sister and brother, the space around me could still be laid out on a map with an abscissa and an ordinate. My old mania of mapping out came back to me like a vague shot of adrenaline. My neighbor was taking a nap now; his head tilted back and in my direction, his eyes covered with a gray mask, his lower jaw lax and his mouth slightly open; I wanted his calm; I would have given anything to sleep. The lights had been dimmed again to a minimum; a discreet fog was coming out of the air vents above us. I stood on my seat, grabbed the headrests on either side and swung my legs and body above my neighbor like on a pommel horse. I was more than a little proud of my prowess. I stood in the pathway waiting for something to happen, for someone to clap. How little the world registered me and my actions surprised me. Of course, it had also delighted me, freed me to do whatever I had fancied without fearing for consequences. As an immigrant, I had winked at random in the metro, forgotten to pay in department stores, attended fencing classes I wasn't registered for, driven across a roundabout in reverse in the dead of night, gone to lie on the wrong side of the bed, washed my hair with dish soap. Those small misdemeanors had helped me to feel alive in a world that I felt so detached from. No one had paid attention. I had.

As I got closer to the bathroom, I overheard a discussion about the number of bathrooms on planes and the shrinking distance between seats. It was sounding far, as if I was listening through a keyhole.

"After you!" someone standing in line by the bathroom said.

I knew the voice before I recognized Anton, my godfather.

He was now next in line on the lavatory doorstep. He was wearing his Sunday checkered shirt and held a steaming cup of coffee. Anton's imposing silhouette always had an anchoring effect on me: I felt grounded, as if the cabin pressure had increased a notch. I stood there and waited beside him; I took the opportunity to correct my posture, performed a few ankle rotations, a neck roll. There was a lapse in my memory. I felt guilty as I had the sacred task of engraving all of the minute details forever. Anton's hair had not always been white, as I thought I remembered. His hair had once been a solid buttered toast shade, except for a few white strands on the temples. There were so few whites, in fact, that they could be counted, but those upset me as if, on this plane, waiting in line for the bathroom, I was meeting for the first time the marks of old age. The lock to the bathroom turned green and someone got out. Anton put his free hand on my shoulder to help me squeeze by, and I relished the weightlessness of his fingers like a skillfully placed rest in a small melody.

I slammed the door behind me. For the moment, I needed away from my dead relatives on the plane. I knew they wouldn't come into the bathroom as I sat there. They were too respectful for that. My dead were a little shy, like me. They wouldn't dare insert themselves in the bathroom cube. The idea might have crossed their minds, but they wouldn't act on it. My family was big on the respect for privacy, which also meant they ran away from raw emotions, from strong gestures of affection, from closed bathrooms. They were essentially chickens.

Chickens! The word made me happy and I felt young all of a sudden, as if there was a porthole behind my back, and the difference in air pressure sucked out the years off of me and into the atmosphere. I wondered what I looked like. I stretched up a bit until I could see the crown of my head in the mirror. My hair was frizzy on top. Jaqui had always said that my hair looked best the second day after washing and this was not it. This felt more like a wig, a fur, something superimposed on my skull. My hair was foreign to me. It scared me. I summoned myself with my old name: Yeti. It also sounded weird: Yeti—Yeti—Yeti. Of course, it was unending: every part of my body, every sound I made was strange, since there was no one I knew under the layers of alienness.

Finally I stood and staggered, avoided looking in the mirror, which was hard given the limited amount of space. I felt lightheaded, I held on the edge of the mini metal sink and slid the door lock at the same time.

One hostess saw me come out and worried; she made me sit on a folding seat in the galley and gave me a drink of water before she left. My aunt Pauli sat across the passage on the other folding seat.

Aunt Pauli's mouth was open and her breath made a va-

por that looked much like dew evaporating from a tree under the morning sun. The more I looked at Aunt Pauli, the
more I became convinced that her breath did not belong to
her, which calmed me. Moments of silence like this healed
like white ointed gauze on a wound. A parade of silences
marched through my head on an erratic time treadmill:
waking up next to my foreign husband—still asleep and a
bit stinky from the night; a train ride to work with three
quiet, dark-skinned commuters; a lunch in my red kitchen
with one friendly fly; a Sunday at dawn on the school playground's swing with Guil; my grandfather in his open casket—the tranquil line of his jaw, his hair showing tracks
of a comb, the velvety cushion beneath his head. That was
it. The velvety cover of the seats on the plane was made of
a fabric identical to the lining of my grandfather's coffin. I
hadn't been able to identify it at first, but now I knew this
with certainty.

"Did you know?" I asked Aunt Pauli.

"Know what?"

"That they used Grandpa's coffin lining as upholstery on
this plane."

"You just figured this out?"

"Yes."

"That's the type of thing that is preferable not to talk about,
darling. Not outside the family anyway. I am so happy to see
you again, Yeti! Tell me about your life out there."

Aunt Pauli had been an intellectual. She had lived in the
rectory next to the old church. Her house looked so much

like her that I had often been tempted to rest my cheeks on its walls. Pauli talked to me as an adult always. She showed me how to grow lettuce in the garden of the priory. Her salad was light green and crisp and juicy under the bite. Inside her bedroom, bookshelves half-collapsed from the weight of monstrous volumes of encyclopedia. More than once, I enclosed myself in her bathroom with one volume—from the time that I had learned to read until I had left for good, I only ever got to the letter D; I had been religiously linear, picking one "letter" volume at a time. People called me a well-behaved child; another me could have led a life of green salad and encyclopedia, perhaps inherited Pauli's rectory.

Now on this plane, looking at Pauli and her apologetic smile, as she waited for me to tell her my life's story, I was surprised at how long I had lived without thinking about her, at how much I had ached for her without knowing it. Pauli once explained that the church had been a simultaneum, meaning several cults were celebrated in it; parishioners had to wait their turn. And I wondered whether I behaved like a "simultaneum" myself, my body enfolding several concurrent "mes" that waited their turn to come out.

All I could recount to Pauli consisted of a description of the apartment I had left behind, of the bakery shop on the ground floor and Madam Val the baker, of my falsely quiet neighborhood, of the bistro where I would stop for red meat and a cocktail at three in the afternoon. It was bizarre to hear myself describing those things as if they were mine and as if they were suddenly coated in a thick layer of nostalgia. It was somebody else talking, and yet that somebody was trying to be detailed and honest. The talking me was unstoppable and beaming. The me that observed the talking me was deeply embarrassed. I was so entrenched in those contradictions that my eyes were wide open without seeing. The space ahead was webbed with lines of thought so dense and resistant that they caught anything extraneous in their way and gobbled it in seconds.

"Madam?"

It was the hostess.

"Do you feel better now?" she asked. "Can I offer you anything?"

"I am fine I think," I said, annoyed by her intrusion, wanting her to go away.

I looked up at Aunt Pauli for support and realized that she had been switched off like a floor lamp.

"I am completely fine. Completely fine." I said to the hostess to gain some time, realizing that this repeated statement may have the opposite effect.

But the hostess left us.

"You should take your pulse," Pauli said "just to be sure."

"Do you think I can take my pulse through my shirt?" I said. "I am really cold. This plane is insanely cold." Something made me not want to roll up my sleeve.

"Well, why don't you just roll up your sleeve for a minute?" Pauli said.

The tattoos appeared there halfway up my forearm. Small letters floating on the surface of my flesh as if they had been freshly copied on tracing paper. I didn't react right away: it took me a while to realize what they were.

Upon my arrival on the other continent, I had been struck by the number of people harboring them; skins turned into indelible parchments out of imperious emotions. I had been vaguely annoyed by them, as if the people with tattoos had pertained to a group that was out of my league, as if they had a shared secret, an unspoken tenet that could only wind up stamped on their hide. On a week day in the metro, one of them had asked me if I had wanted his picture, and I had been very tempted to say yes. He had tattoos on both his forearms; two large-scaled fishes that had looked like they were undulating beneath fresh water toward a hole formed by his rolled-up sleeves. He had spoken with a lot of hand gestures, which had been most encouraging. It had taken a week before the fishes had started undulating in my bed.

I had remained foreign to my lover always, including after I had married him. He had spoken to me slowly and clearly as if I was a bit hard of hearing. He hadn't hesitated to repeat things to make sure I understood. He had wanted babies with names that pertained exclusively to his continent. Names with initials that ended on my forearm. I had tried. It had been exhilarating to love unconceived, unborn babies with hard-to-pronounce names. It had made me stay up at night and look at the small initials and caress them with my other hand. Them: the babies that I never had. I missed them. I missed my husband.

"I can't seem to find my pulse," I said.

"What do you mean?" Aunt Pauli said.

"It looks like you don't have a pulse," someone commented.

I was most unnerved to have lost my pulse.

"It could be anywhere, you know."

I lifted my head and both Jaqui and Guil were standing there, with an air of quiet triumph. The whole passageway was now crammed with my dead relatives. Even my cousin Max had joined the party. I saw him measuring the bewilderment on my face.

"Your pulse: When did you last feel it?" he asked.

"I don't know," I said. "I don't regularly check my pulse."

"Well you should, cuz. Pulses need to be checked often. They need the attention. They can feel neglected and there's the chance that they'll take off."

"Really?"

"Don't worry too much. They usually reappear. They get bored on the outside." Max clicked his tongue.

"It's good to see you, Yeti, even without a pulse," he added.

A lump formed in my throat and the loudspeaker interjected before I could respond.

Ladies and gentlemen, as we start our descent, please return to your seat and make sure your seat backs and tray tables are in their full upright position. Make sure your seat belt is securely

Biographical Note

Cécile Barlier was born in France and received her master's degree from the Sorbonne University in Paris. For over two decades, she has lived in the United States, raising two daughters and working alongside her husband, Pierre, as an entrepreneur. She lives in Lafayette, California. Two of her short stories—"A Gypsy's Book of Revelation" and "Forgetting"—have been nominated for the Pushcart Prize. "Forgetting" was featured in *Epiphany*'s *The Writers Studio at 30* anthology. Barlier won the 2019 Grace Paley Prize for Short Fiction. Barlier's other work has been widely featured (or is forthcoming) in a variety of literary magazines, including *Amarillo Bay*, *Valparaiso Fiction Review*, *Cerise Press*, and *Delmarva Review*.

fastened and all carry-on luggage is stowed underneath the seat in front of you or in the overhead bins. Thank you.

Throughout this last leg of the flight, my dead had persuaded me that this was my last migration, and a normal landing had become an unthinkable development. But I still wandered back to my seat with no conviction, watching the faces of exhausted strangers that seemed oddly friendly. Even my sleepy neighbor stood up to let me sit.

The plane approached a layer of clouds and I had a terrible urge to cry. I wondered where all my people had gone now. Where were they? Would they ever come back and visit? Did I stir them out of their peaceful limbo? Did I hurt them? Or worse. And now it was just me and the man beside me—both of us wearing our seatbelts like we had been instructed. Both of us seated upright, our legs uncrossed and fully awake under the restorative air blown onto us like a morning shower from the vents above.

"Do you have the time?" the man asked.

"I think it is one thirty in the afternoon," I said, looking at my watch and computing the time difference in my head as I pulled the skin on my cheeks with a hand swipe.

"Thank you," he said and I felt him hesitating.

Three seconds passed during which the man gathered his thoughts and looked for the thing he felt he had forgotten.

"It's funny. I thought we would land early in the morning," he said. "Those long flights have a way of disrupting our inner clock."

He had the embarrassed smile of someone who just said a banality as big as himself.

"True," I said.

My neighbor thrusted his upper body forward and down; and he busied himself with his shoelaces for a while. The plane had penetrated the crust of clouds and an ivory cotton mist was padding the outside. What I had called home a million years ago was below the crust, and my mother was waiting there, holding onto her life until I showed up.